Restrained

AN ARROWED SERIES NOVELLA

THE ARROWED SERIES
BOOK 4.5

GRYFFIN MURPHY

"There's something broken about this
But I might be hoping about this
Oh, what a sin."

-Hozier

Author's Note

Dear reader,

This work is a companion to the *Arrowed Series*, following two secondary characters on their journey through the events of the series.

Naturally, this book contains spoilers for the main storyline of the series. Rest assured, it *can* be read as a standalone, but if you have the time to binge a quick, easily-read series, the author suggests diving into Arrowed Books 1-4 for utmost context/enjoyment:

•Arrowed
•Love-Struck
•Quiver
•Pulled

Either way you choose, Happy Reading!

Your pal,
Gryffin

Content Warnings

Restrained is a little more grim than its companion series. For your reading pleasure, it is crucial to acknowledge that some aspects of this narrative may touch upon sensitive subjects, challenging themes, or intense situations, such as:

- Familial abuse/trauma
  - Child Disownment
  - Loss of a parent
  - Motorbike accident
  - Foul language
  - Sexual harassment
  - Jealousy
  - Blood and injury
  - Drug abuse, drug dealing, mentions of overdose
  - Nausea/Vomiting
  - Near-death experiences
  - Mentions of death/murder

PART ONE

The First Year

CHAPTER 1

Connall

My father and I were silent as our car loudly made its way over the gravel road. He had never been one for much conversation, but I still couldn't believe he had nothing to say to me now. In these final moments, whether he liked it or not, I was still his son. I deserved more words than I'd been given:

"You're 19 now," he said, his Irish brogue lacking any emotion, "And ye've not Arrowed, so I'm sending you off to join our brother clan in America."

"Because I haven't Arrowed yet?" I dared to question him. *It wasn't for lack of trying!* For over a year, my lonely heart desperately searched for my soulmate. But no wolves ever looked my way, and the bond that felt like you'd been struck by Cupid's Arrow only formed when you and your destined soulmate connected eyes.

"Arrow on a lass there, and keep our ties strong," he continued.

He said it as if it were something I could just arrange. I thought to speak the protest aloud, but I could hear the finality in his tone.

He didn't intend for me to only visit and determine if, perhaps, my soulmate was American. He expected me to join them for good.

I felt bile rise in the back of my throat. Joining the Montana pack and accepting their Alpha as my own would mean severing all ties from my family and my home. Our minds would no longer share one consciousness in our wolf form, and I would never be susceptible to my father's Alpha commands or hear his thoughts in my head again.

He truly meant to banish me. *Was I that much of a disappointment?*

I finally dared to protest. "Da—"

"Is that wise, *Athair?*" my older brother Ceallach cut in.

For a moment, I let myself believe he was going to defend me, even ask our father to let me stay. Ceallach hadn't Arrowed either, and surely he could call out the unfairness in that.

"What American she-wolf would fall for a sap the like of him?" my brother finished, "The sea wouldn't give Connall a wave."

I *was* a sap compared to my brothers. Growing up, while they threw rocks at each other, I preferred to stack the stones instead, and would cry whenever they knocked my piles over. I once overheard my Uncle Tadgh try to explain the reason for my emotional disposition, theorizing that my mother had given me her entire heart when I entered the world... which was also why my birth caused her death.

My uncle's words were a curse on my image the moment he spoke them, and I was forever thereafter deemed *the runt of the litter.* "Too much milk inside and not enough iron," they'd say, as if giving a care was the worst thing a wolf could do. In a twisted way, it helped my father rationalize his hatred for me. Though he never said it aloud, I knew he blamed me for the loss of his mate.

To appease him, I'd trained myself to bury those weaker parts of me, hidden so deeply inside that my face to the world was forever made of stone. I never revealed anything to anyone, cutting myself off from my emotions for so many years that I could scarcely recognize them within myself.

Even as the car passed the grand iron gates of Wolfsblood Ranch, and my heart began to race, my face remained stony and unmoving. I stared out the window, trying to take in the views of my new home. Montana was beautiful, but it was nothing compared to the Irish countryside I was leaving behind.

The sound of a loud motor overtook the car, and a small figure on a large motorbike sped past us. For a moment, I was worried that I'd flinched at the sudden sound, but having not heard a grunt of disapproval from my dad, I determined I must've only blinked in reaction.

Resting my forehead to the window, I watched as the bike moved faster ahead of us. I felt pulled to it, wanting to ask our driver to follow the motorcyclist and see where they were going in such a hurry. In a rare stroke of luck, it ended up being the same destination: the house of the American pack's Alpha, an impressive home on the expansive ranch.

We exited the car, and I took in the vision of the bike rider dismounting, pleasantly surprised to discover it was a beautiful young woman. She appeared to be around my age, with dark and wildly curly hair piled atop her head. After such a ride, many tendrils had broken free and curled around her face.

I envied those curls, wanting to orbit around her beauty as they did.

She moved toward the barn by the house, pausing suddenly to eye us over her shoulder as if she'd caught on to my staring. I couldn't feel any embarrassment over that, too thrilled to simply be noticed by her.

Look at me, I mentally begged. *Please look me in the eyes.*

I stepped forward, a rare hope rising in my chest. If *she* were my soulmate, exile here might not be so bad.

"You don't wear a helmet?" I asked, trying harder for her attention.

"Christ, Connall," my dad groaned, "Leave her be."

The girl turned around and fully looked at me, her green eyes bright but somewhat menacing, like the shade of a viper snake.

I was captivated by her eyes... but I did not Arrow.

"I'm not as delicate as I look," she said, raising a dark eyebrow. Her voice had a delicious rasp that scratched all my senses.

"You'll have to excuse my son," my father said, coming around from his side of the car, "*He's* more delicate than he looks."

I felt my neck warm with embarrassment and abandoned all hope. Pulling my eyes from hers, I silently walked beside my dad toward the Alpha's house, wishing I had just started the conversation by asking for the girl's name.

The front door opened, and a middle-aged woman with a friendly smile stepped onto the front porch.

"Colm, Connall, welcome!" she greeted us, "How was the trip?"

"Hello, Adeline," my father replied quite stiffly, "Shall we begin?"

Her eyebrows shot up in surprise. "Don't you want any coffee, tea, or perhaps a ceremonial welcome whiskey first?" Her eyes flicked between the two of us. "I'm sure it was a long journey here."

My father released a harsh burst of air through his nostrils. "Aye, and it's a long journey back. So—sooner, the better."

I swallowed at his brusqueness, my throat thickening.

"Very well." Adeline nodded and politely gestured for us to follow her. As we made it into the foyer, she linked her arm with mine. I was surprised by the comforting gesture and worried it meant she could see the dread that was storming beneath my hardened exterior. "Your father tells me you're excited to come to America," she spoke to me with something on the edge of her tone. *Doubt, perhaps.*

"Aye, ma'am," I murmured dutifully.

She looked at me with deep consideration before turning her attention to my father. "I don't want your trip to have been needless, Colm, but as I said on the phone... We've always been honest with each other. We haven't had an Arrow occur on the ranch in some time."

"Aye, I know," he replied, "But as *I* said on the phone, perhaps some new blood might aid in that. 'Tis not rare for a member of my family to emigrate and join yours, and vice versa."

"Well, sure, but rarely are they so young—"

"I was very sorry to hear of Killian's passing." His words cut her off.

"Thank you," she replied, not missing a beat, "I'm grateful for your steadfast support. It's not been easy stepping into my husband's shoes."

"You needn't worry about that; your boy is coming of age soon." It was a blatant snub to her for having questioned him.

My muscles flexed, bringing her arm a small distance closer to me in apology. In this short conversation, she had shown more grace and diplomacy as an Alpha than I'd ever seen my father display in the nineteen years of knowing him.

"Indeed," she replied unshakingly, "Shall we?"

Without further ado, she led us out the door to her backyard and beyond to the backwoods, where we shifted a safe distance from each other in the trees. The moment I became a wolf, and my consciousness melded with my father's, I fought hard to keep my thoughts quiet. My father's mind in wolf form was always so animalistic, and he hated hearing my "useless ramblings" in his head. Perhaps that alone was reason enough for banishment: It mattered little that I revealed no feelings to the world. The fact that I felt *anything* inside at *all* was still a crime against the family.

Stand beside her, boy, his order echoed in my mind.

I obliged, padding over to sit beside our host and face him head-on. Adeline bowed her head lowly, as did he. I was not given any instruction to do the same, and so I remained still and upright as he began reciting the traditional words used for the ceremony. As his intonations pierced through my thoughts, I took the time to survey him, quietly wondering if this was the last time I would ever see him. It was such an odd dichotomy to be facing a beast who never wanted me around and yet still feel panicked at the thought of losing him.

Do you accept? he concluded.

It mattered little what he had said before the question. I knew there was only one acceptable answer.

I accept, I swore in my mind, and the magic of the words took effect. My mind severed its connection from my father's and bonded with Adeline's, my new Alpha.

It felt like being pushed off a cliff, only to be caught by someone's hand in the final moment, a terrifying lurch that sent my stomach plummeting before it rebounded back again.

As I looked upon my father with no connection remaining between us, I felt empty. I imagined it was how he'd always wanted me to feel. If only he could sense it, he might have felt proud. Instead, he turned and ran out of the woods.

If he had any last words to say, I couldn't hear them.

I might have felt inclined toward feelings of devastation, were it not for the unusual warmth that began to fill my chest.

You will have a home here, Connall, Adeline spoke.

It was a shock to my system to hear a new voice in my mind, but as I turned to her, I felt comforted by the softness in her eyes.

She bent her head with respect. *I cannot guarantee you a soulmate,* she continued, *but I can guarantee you a family. Welcome to Wolfsblood.*

CHAPTER 2

Frankie

I held up the rusted hood with one hand as I inspected the mechanics of our latest repair project: an *actual, real-life* truck. My cousin Noah and I had successfully built my bike with junkyard parts, and it was his equally dumb and bold idea to take it a step further and miraculously master the mechanics of four-wheeled vehicles.

Instead of doing much surveying of the machinery, however, my eyes glassed over, too preoccupied with thoughts of our mysterious new pack member. Connall had been with us for about a month, and I still couldn't bring myself to say any more words to him than I had on his very first day.

I kept replaying the moment my eyes first saw him:

He had a pale face and a structured jaw, and were it not for his bright red hair, I would've sworn he was a marble statue. *And that accent.*

An involuntary shiver went down my spine, a cruel reminder to reject those thoughts of him. In every pack meeting, I had to struggle to think of anything else other than how the rumbling of his voice vibrated the butterflies in my stomach. I would muse about school, motorbikes, my annoying little brother, *anything* to keep the pack from hearing how obsessed I was becoming with Connall.

Or how I desperately wished something special had happened when I first saw him.

I wanted to hate him for making me feel so silly and girlish with a crush. Our kind was not meant to yearn for anyone other than our destined soulmate.

I shook my head and shut the hood, telling myself for the umpteenth time to get a grip. We hadn't Arrowed, and that was that. We were forbidden from any romantic activity with anyone but our mate... *unless you were the Alpha's son, of course, and could get away with breaking the rules.*

"Where have *you* been?" I asked my cousin Noah, the heir himself, as he dragged his feet into the barn.

He ran a hand through his mop top head of curls, which were long overdue for a trim. "With Chloe," he said, his voice grim.

If *he* knew that *I* knew he was dating outside the bond, neither of us acknowledged it. He was just as careful as I was in controlling his wolf thoughts. I was certain his mother had no idea what he got up to with his witch friend when no one was watching.

"I invited Connall to help us. Has he shown up yet?" he asked, pulling me from my speculation.

I swallowed harshly. "You did *what?*"

"The guy just lost his connection to his entire family, Frances. The least we could do is offer to be his friend."

My uncle's passing was still a fresh wound for Noah, and I could see how he felt for someone who'd also lost their father in a way. Even so, I wasn't about to allow the greatest of dangers into my only safe space on the ranch.

"Do *not* call me Frances," I ordered, "And find something else to do with him. I'm not letting some random wolf put his paws on *our* project."

"No worries," Connall said from the doorway, evidently having arrived just in time to hear my dismissal.

I felt the blood drain from my face and pool in my chest with embarrassment.

"Oh hey, man!" Noah greeted him warmly, "Glad you could make it."

"Conan, is it?" I asked, trying to play it cool.

"Connall," he corrected softly.

"Don't be a bitch, Frances," Noah scolded through his teeth.

I turned and punched my cousin's arm as hard as I could. "I *said*, don't *call me that!*"

Connall just stood there, his face revealing nothing.

I could have died from the embarrassment. "I'm sorry, I wasn't trying to... be a bitch," I said weakly. I could barely stand to meet his gaze for a second before I had to tear my eyes away.

"Yeah, ignore her," Noah added lightly, "We all do."

"Sure, ignore me." I gave up, brushing past them both on my way out the door. "You guys have fun."

All it took was for one more guy to show up, and I was kicked out of the boys' club. Clenching my fists, I moved to mount my bike, thinking a quick ride might help with my increasing frustration. The last thing I needed to do was rage-shift and come off like some novice wolf who wasn't in control of herself.

"Didja build that yerself?" Connall asked, following me.

"We both did," Noah answered proudly, "We're teaching ourselves in the hopes to run a full shop someday. It would save the ranch some money if we could repair things ourselves."

"Do they cover that at your school?" Connall's attention remained on me.

I looked away for a moment, softly grinning in a private celebration. *Seems like Noah's the one getting ignored now.* "No," I replied, turning back around, "We're self-taught, which really just means we have no idea what we're doing. Are you enrolling at the college?"

"That's what I'm told."

My heart raced at the sound of his brogue and the way he stared at me so intently. While I could barely bring myself to look at him, it seemed almost as if *I* was the only thing *he* could focus on. "You'll have to lose the accent a bit," I advised him, "Learn to sound more like a local to avoid too many questions."

"They told me that too."

I met Connall's gaze once more, feeling a shock go down my spine. We were wordless for a moment, just looking at each other. The more we stared the harder it became to look away. I felt as though my entire world was spinning off its axis, and I almost forgot my idiot cousin was a witness to this electrifying stand-off occurring between us.

"Is the tantrum over? Can we get back to work now?" Noah pleaded as he leaned against the barn entryway. "I'm sorry I told him to ignore you." He redirected his attention to Connall, "You can't ignore her, Connall."

As his head turned, I could see the back of Connall's neck became unusually red. "What?" he asked, "I wasn't— I wouldn't—"

"It isn't possible," Noah continued forebodingly, "She *cannot* be ignored. She'll just keep wailing and wailing until the entire town thinks it's a siren for a tornado."

I threw my head back and groaned. *Would he ever stop trying to embarrass me?!* "You are such an ass!" I yelled, abandoning my bike to run at him.

"Hear how that sounded?" Noah called out to Connall, covering his ears with wince before he evaded my attack, "I bet the neighbors are running to shelter as we speak!"

Connall just stood there with a stoic expression as he watched me chase Noah around the truck. Sensing his lack of amusement, I stopped my pursuit and tried to compose myself.

"Sorry. We act like morons sometimes," I lamented, "I'm sure you'd rather hang out anywhere else."

Connall didn't disagree as he looked down. "I should probably leave you guys to it," he murmured.

"Aw, that's okay, man, I—" Noah's words faltered as Connall turned and walked away.

I waited until he was out of earshot before I resumed my pursuit, finally succeeding in tackling Noah to the ground.

"Way to go, idiot, you scared him away," I grunted, moving to punch his shoulder, "Can't you act cool for *one minute?*"

"Me? *You're* the one who kicked him out!" He shoved me off of him and sat up on his hands with a pensive frown. "It's too bad he isn't interested in helping. I have no idea what he likes to do for fun. He doesn't seem like the type that smiles easily."

"No," I agreed, privately wishing there was something I could do to fix that, "He doesn't."

Noah moved to look under the hood, and I stood off to the side, pretending to be busy reading a workshop manual. I smiled down at the words I was failing to read, remembering how thrilling it had been to have Connall's undivided attention for a short moment.

Even if I had been more focused on my reading, I would not have achieved much progress since our friend Milo arrived at the barn shortly thereafter.

His eyes scoped the area, and he looked severely disappointed to see it was only us two inside. "Where's our new friend?" He crossed his tanned arms in admonishment as if he already knew what we'd done.

"Frankie raised her arms, and the stench from her pits sent him running," Noah replied.

I closed my eyes, too bored of his jabs to even roll my eyes. "Or maybe he feared his brain cells depleting just being around the one marble you've got rolling around your skull."

"Or *maybe*," Milo echoed, gesturing between the two of us, "This dynamic did not bode well for a welcoming environment."

"Oh, *our bad*. We were waitin' on you to start the trust falls, Captain." My sarcasm was thick. Milo had been ambling to help with the team-building exercises for company retreats, and it was clear his research on motivational speaking was bleeding into his daily life.

"He has siblings, doesn't he?" Noah recalled, shuffling his foot against the dirt floor, "I'm sure he's used to a 'familial dynamic.'"

"Wait, what? He has *siblings?*" I asked, the horror seeping in.

"His connection was torn from *everybody,*" Milo sympathized.

"Why?!" I demanded, turning to Noah. He was the one most likely to have the full story. "Everyone else who transfers from the Irish pack is either old or settled with a mate and family of their own! Why him?"

"Apparently," Noah lowered his voice, "His dad wanted him to Arrow on someone *here.*"

I didn't enjoy how my stomach flipped at the news. *He had come here to find his mate?* My excitement plummeted at the realization that his fated person clearly wasn't me.

Milo's brows furrowed. "You can't *arrange* a shifter's bond. Even if there was a chance his soulmate was here, it makes no sense to completely change packs before knowing that for a fact. He could've just come to stay for the summer."

"Exactly. *And* Colm *knew* we haven't had an Arrow occur in a while," Noah continued conspiratorially, "Ma told him repeatedly, and he still insisted on bringing Connall to live here. I think the real truth is Connall got into some kind of trouble, and his Alpha determined it was best for the pack to wipe their hands clean of him."

"No way," Milo disagreed, "You've seen inside Connall's mind. He's stoic and intimidating, sure, but he's a gentle giant."

"Nothing he could have done warrants a punishment like that," I added.

"I don't know, you guys." Noah shrugged. "Just feels like there has to be more to it. '*Still waters run deep,*' or whatever they say."

Milo sighed. "We just have to get to know him better."

I looked out towards the path Connall had walked down, our curious questions echoing in my mind. He was one seductive mystery, that was for sure. If anyone would crack that marble and discover what was hidden underneath, I wanted it to be me.

CHAPTER 3

Frankie

G one were my summers of freedom, apparently. I was 17 and expected to contribute to the family business now. My mom and dad had ambushed me, laying out all the opportunities on the ranch's summer schedule and insisting I had to pick *something* to do, just like my friends had. Milo was thrilled to get assigned to shifts at the ropes course, and Noah seemed satisfied with leading horseback riding lessons.

Apparently, I was the only one resenting that our careers had already been decided for us when we hadn't even gone to college yet.

Just because I was a member of the pack, it shouldn't mean every aspect of my life was predetermined. I wasn't certain I would *ever* want to work at Wolfsblood. Hospitality was never an interest nor a strength of mine. The only thing that made me happy was my work in the garage, repairing the things others had discarded and giving them a second life.

When I tried to argue that point, my parents made it clear they didn't believe Noah and I could build a business from what we were doing. Neither could I, *yet*, but it hurt all the same to see their lack of faith in us.

Before they could stop me, I ran out of the house, hopped

onto my motorbike, and kicked it into gear, determined to get as far away from the conversation as I could.

Since I met a certain Irishman, I'd developed a habit of riding far and fast, pretending for just a moment that I truly had the option to get away. I would imagine I'd go somewhere so far that I could outrun my thoughts of him, and Adeline couldn't call me back with an Alpha command.

My intense crush on Connall was a plague that infected every part of me. As if it weren't embarrassing enough that I was unable to act normal around him, I was more conscious of my appearance at all times, hoping to look *pretty*. It was never something I'd cared about, but now, every morning, I would obsess over outfit options, opting for more color than my usual black and denim in case it might catch his eye. My infatuation even changed the music I listened to. While my family knew me to be a fan of loud emo and rock, in the privacy of my room, I started listening to acoustic songs by girls with guitars who sang lyrics that rang true to every ardent thought I had about him. I would play these heartbreak ballads through my headphones, lie on my back in bed, and replay that first moment we met over and over— each time picturing a world in which we *had* Arrowed, and he was mine.

I desperately wondered if my obsession with him would ever stop. Before Connall came to the ranch, I wouldn't have imagined these types of thoughts could even be possible outside the bond. It didn't seem fair. I once thought to ask Noah what it was like with Chloe, if it at all felt the same, but the risk was too great. No one could ever know the extent of my feelings for Connall.

As I increased my bike's speed and approached the main road, I noticed the object of all my desires walking casually along the length of the fence.

I should have known. It was as if my heart had an uncanny ability to find him at all times and unconsciously sought him out.

His head was down, and he focused on the paperback he held in one hand, his other hand tucked into his pocket. He looked so casual and unassuming that one might have looked right past him, missing the glorious vision of his red hair shining in the sun.

If he took notice of *me*, if he even heard me coming, he didn't indicate it.

As I turned the corner, I revved the engine and increased my speed to try to get his attention. I passed him quickly, and in a moment of great stupidity, I glanced over my shoulder to see if I had succeeded in getting him to acknowledge me. The moment my eyes were off the path ahead, I somehow lost control. The scrambler went out from under me, and I cursed loudly as I lurched forward. Before I could brace myself, I crashed to the ground and my body flew across the gravelly pavement. Pebbles and stones ripped my skin open with a burning heat.

"Frankie?!" I heard him yell.

I barrel-rolled to a stop and lay limp in the center of the road, the pain overwhelming.

Don't cry, don't cry, don't cry. I gritted my teeth and damned my tears to hell as I heard him run over to me. *Well, shit, Frankie! He sure noticed you now!*

Before I could grunt another obscenity, I felt warm hands gently roll me onto my back.

"Are you okay?" Connall demanded, moving his arm to support my neck. "Is anything broken? Should I call a doctor?"

I stared up at him in wonder, taking in the most handsomely sculpted expression of concern I'd ever seen. *Maybe I had died, and this was some archangel cradling me...*

His eyes widened with more worry, and my fantasy came crashing back to Earth.

"I'm, like, so fine." I weakly rasped, cringing with equal pain and embarrassment. In the short time I had known him, I had never once seen him display so much emotion. I had also never received this much physical contact from him.

"You are *not* fine," he insisted, his tone unusually flustered, "Your legs are torn to shreds. Shouldn't you be wearing pants to ride this thing?"

I didn't need to look at my legs to know he was right. I felt the sting of all my wounds exposed to the air. "I'll heal."

"We have to clean you up before that happens," he insisted.

Suddenly, I was up in his arms, and he was running us to the ranch's Main Building. I moved my hand to his shoulder, blushing even harder at the spectacle we were making of ourselves.

"What about my bike?" I asked, looking behind us as he slowed, nearing the front stairs.

"I'll go back for it later," he muttered through his teeth, "That ruddy thing could rust on the side of the road for all I care."

"Hey, I made that!" I protested, "That's my baby!"

"And yer baby almost killed ya right in front of my eyes."

"Your accent's slipping," I mumbled grumpily, sneaking another look at his face while his eyes were set ahead. It was entirely ridiculous how strong his jawline was, particularly as the muscles flexed when he ground his teeth in anger.

We entered the lobby and moved up the side stairs to the second floor, thankfully with few witnesses. "Did you hit your head?" he asked, forcing his accent back to the stilted American he'd been practicing.

"I think my limbs took the brunt of it," I answered honestly, "Why?"

"Because you're looking at me like you're having difficulty thinking."

I jolted, squirming to move away from his clutches. "Shut up!"

His grip on me remained firm despite my protests, trapping me up against him like a vice. "I'm serious, Frankie. If you have a concussion, we need to—"

"My head is fine!" *It's my heart that's to blame for my staring.*

He gently set me down on the ground then, and I sat up against the wall by the supply closet, crossing my arms as I watched him unlock the door and begin to search the shelves for a first aid kit.

"Hey, how come you have a key?" I wondered aloud.

"Maggie gave me a copy," he explained, "I asked her what I

could help with around here, and she said I could start manning the boat house at the lake."

"You *want* to work here?"

"Of course. I'm very grateful for the opportunity to contribute and be of some use."

I stared at the floor, feeling guilty for acting like such a brat to my parents. Once Connall retrieved the box of bandages, he looked down at me, his mouth twisting in thought.

"You do *not* need to carry me again," I insisted, moving to stand. *I had to retain some semblance of dignity.* Unfortunately, my legs screamed in pain from the movement, and the moment I was vertical, they gave out completely. I fell forward, colliding with his chest.

"I don't, do I?" he asked, his voice barely a whisper.

I felt another onslaught of embarrassment seep across my chest as I tried to straighten myself out. One leg definitely hurt worse than the other, and I could lean on the better one to limp my way out of the hallway.

He wrapped a tentative arm around my waist, guiding me into an open conference room and helping me sit up on the table inside. His hands were on me for just a second, but once more, I felt myself lit aflame from the brief contact.

Pulling up a chair before me, he sat and opened the kit, cleaning me up with a heavy concentration.

"Where did you learn to do this?" I asked as he sanitized a small pair of tweezers.

"My brothers got into bad scrapes all the time," he explained, "One of us had to learn to be a proper healer, or they'd be covered in scarred skin and bumpy like gourds."

"Are *my* legs going to scar like that?" I jolted in alarm.

He blinked repeatedly as his eyes dragged their way up and down the extent of the damage. "Not if I can help it. You should wear pants on your bike from now on, though. And a helmet."

I frowned. "I told you, I didn't hit my head."

"You hit *everythin*," he corrected, his accent slipping on the final word, "I saw the whole thing happen. How did you crash, anyway? I thought you were quite skilled on a bike."

"A bug hit my neck," I lied terribly as I laid on my back to avoid his eyes. "I just flinched, and that was it."

He was silent for a moment, and I prayed that he would just believe the lame story and drop it. "This is going to sting," he warned me when he finally spoke.

I stiffened in preparation, fighting the urge to hiss through my teeth when he made contact with the first scrape and began to clean out the gravel embedded in my skin.

"Maybe ride around on four wheels for a while," he said softly to distract me.

"Are you this bossy with everyone, or just me because I'm a girl?" I sat up with the accusation. That was one pet peeve that might *(hopefully)* cure me of the crush.

He looked up at me in surprise. "No one has ever accused me of being bossy before."

"So it *is* personal. I must be blessed." I rolled my eyes and laid back down. "*Forced* to be the only 'she-wolf' amongst *boys*. *Cursed* to forever be treated differently, like I'm the weaker sex, when— I'll have you know— my wolf could probably run *miles* around you all."

"That's not it," he insisted quietly.

"Then what is it? Why do you care so much if my legs get scraped up? I can handle it."

"Because," he answered quickly, his accent returning, "I happen to have a high affinity for your legs, and I'd hate to tarnish the view."

My eyes bulged, but I continued to stare at the ceiling, unable to check and see if he was serious. My chest felt hot and my ears were almost ringing in panic. Maybe I was concussed after all, because it was otherwise pathetic that a simple compliment would send me into such a tailspin. *Unless... was he flirting?*

I grinned at the possibility my obsession wasn't so one-sided.

"Frankie," he murmured, his tone having some unknown emotion behind it.

"Tell me more about your brothers," I changed the subject. If he already regretted giving me the compliment, I didn't want to know.

CHAPTER 4

Connall

After Frankie's scrapes were disinfected and her legs were wrapped in gauze to hold the antibiotic ointment against her skin, I insisted she remain on the table until she had fully healed.

In a strange way, I just had to see the proof of her healed legs to be satisfied she would be okay. That, and I was practically drunk off having so much time alone with her. I was insatiable in my desire for Frankie's company. I wanted to be around her all the time.

In the short moments we'd shared, she never made me feel expected to act in any certain way. The other pack members were always so friendly, and I could see they wished for me to return their warmth in a way I was ill-equipped to. With Frankie and her entertainingly gruff personality, I didn't have to force any pleasantries. I could just be. Even as I sat before her, I found I could speak freely for the first time in my life. I was even able to talk candidly about my brothers.

"They sound like assholes," she replied when I'd finished a long story, the most words I might have strung together in years. "And, terrible brothers."

"They're great wolves," I spoke quietly. *Better than me.*

"Being cruel does not make you a great wolf," she disagreed with a dismissive sneer, "A great wolf protects their pack."

"I know you're protective of your little brother." It was one of the first things I noticed about her mind when we first shifted. Whenever he acted out, if anyone had a disparaging thought against him that went too far, she would pounce. I had never experienced that kind of loyalty or *fiercely* protective love, and it struck me in the chest any time I witnessed it.

"Benji's annoying, but his heart is in the right place," she said.

"He's never bothered me," I promised.

"You really should've seen Noah and Milo when they were his age. They were *so* much worse. Consider yourself lucky you didn't come sooner."

The corners of my mouth twitched, and I looked down at my lap. "I can imagine," I murmured, picturing what my life might have been like if I had shared years with her, growing up alongside her.

It was as if she read my mind when she then asked, "What were you like growing up?"

I couldn't lie to her. "Very uncool. Bit of an *eejit*, really."

"I find that hard to believe," she murmured.

"What're you two doing?" a loud voice came from the doorway.

We turned to find Maggie, my new boss, in the doorway.

"I fell," Frankie said confidently, lifting her legs to show off her bandages. "Connall was just helping."

"Okay, well, get off the table. You'll scuff the wood with your sneakers. And don't hang around this room, it's for guests only!" She had quite the talent for scolding. "Not to mention, you two shouldn't be alone. Find something useful to do. *Separately.*" Emphatically, she then gestured for us to leave.

"I'm sorry. We'll go." I stood and held out my hands in anticipation of helping Frankie, but she came down from the table on her own and walked straight past Maggie with her head held high.

As we made our way down the hallway, and I felt Maggie's eyes watch us leave, a deep shame overwhelmed me. I didn't want Maggie to think I was already abusing the privilege of having a set of keys.

"She acts as if we need a chaperone," Frankie muttered through her teeth once we were a safe distance away.

"She's right," I disagreed, "We shouldn't be alone."

"Like hell we shouldn't!" she snapped, "Am I not allowed to have any male friends just because I'm a girl? That's so medieval."

Once again, the corners of my mouth mysteriously twitched. *We were friends?*

"Come on, let's get my bike back to the barn," she continued, marching forward, "No one will bother us there."

My heart rate increased with excitement at her words, but my hopes plummeted when Milo intervened, approaching us in the lobby.

"Is that your bike in the middle of the road?" he asked Frankie.

"It is," she replied, crossing her arms. "And?"

"And it's in the middle of the road," he repeated. "Didn't you know? You can't park there."

"You're hilarious." Her voice was dripping with sarcasm, and she brushed his shoulder with hers as she continued walking. She paused to look at me when she sensed I wasn't beside her anymore. "You gonna follow me?"

I just might, forever. "I—"

"What are you guys up to?" Milo looked between the two of us. "I think I was annoying my dad too much in the kitchen because he ordered me to go help my mom."

"She's in a mood today," Frankie warned him. "We just saw her."

"Well then, if I *just so happen* to get pulled away by some *other* task, I wouldn't mind." He turned to me with a smile. "What do you feel like doing, bro?"

I was unable to offer up any ideas, as I wasn't used to being asked such a thing. As I looked down at my hands, I winced in embarrassment. "I have to return this first aid kit to the closet," I said lamely, holding it up. "I didn't mean to take it." *I'd been too distracted by the company beside me.*

"I suppose that means my fate is sealed," Milo said with a fake sigh. "Save yourself, Frankie. Connall and I will take one for the team and face my mother's wrath alone."

Before Frankie could say a word, Milo clapped his hand on my shoulder and directed us to walk back up the stairs. We moved in silence for a short moment before he caught me eyeing Frankie's departure from over my shoulder. "If Frankie's ever short with you, please don't take it personally," he warned me. "She's more of a black cat than a wolf, but she means well."

"Black cat?" I repeated. *As in, a sign of bad luck?*

"Yeah," he said with a nod, "Picture a sassy—maybe even a little feral— black barnyard cat. She just skulks around her machines in the barn, and if you try to show her affection, she'll get overwhelmed and scratch you. But, if you give her space, eventually, she'll come out from her corner and want to hang out with you. In fact, someday, she might even insist upon your company."

I nodded, the corners of my eyes crinkling at the imagery. "I see."

"I was adopted into the pack from another country too, y'know," he said after another pause, "I was a baby at the time, but I can relate to sometimes feeling like an outsider in this tiny Montana town. If you ever feel like talking..."

"Thanks. I appreciate that." I could see how much effort he was making, but I couldn't bring myself to match his energy.

He stopped walking and eyed me with suspicion. "I'm beginning to suspect... Maybe you're like a cat, too?"

Whatever Frankie was, I was more than happy to be categorized as the same. "Maybe I am."

"Then I'll give you space for a little longer," he replied lightly, resuming his strides, "But just know... none of us will go too far. We've determined we like you a lot, and once you're a part of our friend group, there's no getting out of it."

He'd jokingly phrased it as a threat, but I silently hoped he was serious.

Later that evening, I saw the truth behind his promise. As I entered the kitchen of the Main Building to retrieve some dinner and return to my cabin, Noah and Milo were already there. They greeted me warmly and assumed I would be joining them in the eating hall without a question.

"Noah, you grab a table and I'll take our plates," Milo offered, swiftly pulling my meal from my hands the moment I finished my tour of the buffet. He nodded to me. "You wanna grab our drinks? Coke for me."

"Same!" Noah yelled from over his shoulder as he exited through the swinging doors.

Dutifully, I moved to fountain machine to fill three cups with soda. When I made it through the doors, I saw Milo and Noah hadn't gotten too far. They had paused right by the kitchen entryway to chat with Frankie.

I nearly stumbled and spilled our drinks just from seeing her again so soon.

"Hey!" she protested playfully, shoving her cousin, "You beat me!"

"We have to if there is any hope for us to get any food," Noah countered, "Your stomach is a black hole."

"You guys," Milo murmured, as if referencing a prior conversation I wasn't privy to.

"How are ya?" I asked her in the brief pause that followed. My eyes drifted down to her smooth legs that were no longer bandaged.

"Good as new," she said lightly, bevelling her foot in emphasis, "Though, I can't say the same for my bike."

"What happened to your bike?" Noah asked with immense curiosity, his eyes moving between the two of us.

"Nothing we can't fix," she answered immediately. She gave me a pointed look to let me know it was not a story her cousin was meant to hear. As the other two turned to continue their hunt for a table, she reached out a hand to keep me from following them. "Not that he would tattle," she spoke quietly, "but I can't risk Noah telling my parents that I fell off my bike. They hate my baby enough as it is."

I felt the back of my neck warm and the corner of my mouth twitch. I liked the idea of having a secret with her. It felt... *exciting*.

"Just between us, then," I promised.

She flashed a grin, and I felt my eyes drift down to her smile. Perhaps it was my lack of experience in talking to unspeakably attractive girls, but I suddenly couldn't find it in me to look away from her mouth. I felt so drawn to her lips I had to plant my heels to keep myself from leaning in any closer and—

I realized she was holding her breath, and my eyes immediately returned to hers with sheepish regret, wondering if I'd made her uncomfortable with my imposing stare.

When our eyes re-connected, however, it felt like I'd been struck by lightning. Her pupils were dilated, her gaze mirroring whatever desire displayed in my own. There was no mating bond to speak of, but I knew then for certain that whatever it was developing between us, she, too, felt affected by it.

"Just between us," she echoed.

PART TWO

The Second Year

CHAPTER 5

Connall

After months of pining and waiting, the day had finally arrived: Frankie's 18th birthday. It was the only rope pulling me forward, the thought that maybe we'd not yet Arrowed on each other simply because she was two years younger than me and hadn't been the typical age for the bond when we'd met.

In the year I'd come to know Frankie, I realized I couldn't imagine any soulmate who could be *better*. She was so full of fire in all the ways I was smoke, bringing a warmth and light to the hazy darkness within me. I tried to form the habit of only seeing her as a friend, to respect the laws of our kind, but then there would be moments when I would pluck a leaf to press in a book, simply because it matched the color of her eyes, or I'd wake from a dream with her raspy voice still echoing in my mind, and I would know I had failed.

Her music echoed loudly outside the barn, and as I neared it, I could see her hips shaking back and forth, the rest of her completely immersed under the hood of what would soon be Noah's truck. They'd made great strides in fixing it, and it was almost ready for its first test drive.

"Happy Birthday," I murmured as I stepped into the light,

hiding my gift behind my back.

She turned, an excited smile on her face. The moment our gaze connected, however, her face faltered. Apart from the usual jolt in my ribs that I felt when looking into her eyes, nothing more happened between us.

"Fuck," she swore, turning back to her work. "I mean, um, you scared me."

"Ye've got quite the mouth on you, you know that?" I wondered aloud, pushing through the disappointment that weighed heavily on my heart.

"Oh, please pardon my French, Con," she retorted sarcastically, "You should watch *your* mouth— your accent's slipping."

"I feel like I *pardon your French* quite often," I commented, forcing myself to sound American, "I may just start calling you French."

She wiped the grease from her hands, turning to face me with an amused half-smile. "Do what you'd like, but only if no one else catches on and starts using it too."

I laid a hand over my heart with the promise. "Just between us." Since we first said the phrase, it had become a repeated vow of sorts, a mantra reaffirming all the secrets that we agreed to hold for each other since the very first one we shared.

She looked at me sincerely, some unknown emotion in her eyes. "Just between us."

As I dropped my hand, she regrettably caught sight of the other one hidden behind my back.

"Is that a gift for me?" she asked, her tone very sweet as she took a step toward me.

I felt my neck warm. "Just something small. I don't venture off the ranch much to get a feel for the nearby shops, nor would I pretend to know what any girl wants for her 18th birthday..."

She held out a hand expectantly. "Let's see how you did."

My stomach twisted as I placed the small satchel into her hand.

She raised an eyebrow in curious surprise and twisted her mouth to hide her smile. Carefully, she opened the small drawstring bag and turned it over, dropping the golden Claddagh ring into her palm.

I'd been thinking when I gave the ring to her it'd be as a proposal after Arrowing. Now, facing her silent stare at her hand, I realized it was an inappropriate gift since we had not. Even so, I wanted her to have it.

"It's a Claddagh," I explained, "If you wear it with the heart facing one way, it means your heart is open."

"What if my heart isn't open?" she asked, her tone withholding.

I took a deep, steadying breath. "When you Arrow, you can flip it the other way."

"That wasn't what I meant." She closed her fist around the ring and dropped her hand to her side, not putting it on.

"If you don't like it, I'll gladly take it back from ye," I offered immediately.

"I didn't say I didn't like it." She took a bold step closer, scanning my face.

"W-what are you doing?" I could scarcely breathe from the proximity.

"Saying thank you," she murmured, her eyes dropping to my mouth.

No! I thought I heard my father's voice in my head for the first time in over a year. As much as I wanted to kiss her, I couldn't deny his imminent outrage over the notion that I'd crossed the line with someone who wasn't my mate.

"No thanks needed," I said, taking a step back and lowering my eyes.

"Connall," Frankie prodded softly.

I blinked, wishing I could just close my eyes completely and savor the sound of her saying my name in that tone.

She took advantage of my hesitation and grabbed my shoulders, pulling me to her. With weakened knees, I stumbled forward, but she caught me easily and her arms wrapped around me tightly. She buried her head in my neck as she pushed her body flush against mine. It was all I could do not to let out a groan at the feeling of all of her lining up so perfectly with all of me.

I couldn't remember the last time I'd been hugged like this— if there ever even was a time— yet somehow, after a small pause, my limbs knew what to do. Unconsciously, I wrapped my arms around her waist, leaning my head to rest against hers.

If she intended to hold me for long, I didn't know and found I didn't care. I wouldn't be the one letting go anytime soon.

"What the hell is going on here?" Noah asked from behind us.

Frankie pulled away, and the air between us chilled from where her warmth had just occupied. "Nothing," she said with forced nonchalance, "I was just thanking Connall for my birthday gift."

"That looked a lot more than nothing to me," Noah pressed, "In fact, it looked like crossing a line."

"That's fucking rich, coming from you," she sneered.

"French," I murmured. She needn't get in such a row with her cousin over me. He was right. We'd been dangerously toeing the line.

"Yes, Frankie, *I know what I'm talking about*," he retorted, "There are consequences to breaking the rules, okay? I had to learn that the hard way!"

"We were *just hugging!*" she stepped up to him. As much as I hated seeing her upset, it was a marvel to watch her go toe-to-toe with the other wolves. She never once shied away from a fight. "What *you've* done is a lot fucking worse!"

"French," I said, a little louder this time.

Noah turned his attention to me with a sneer. "And what about you, man? What are *you* doing? What would *your dad*—"

I didn't know what came over me, but I was on him before he could say another word. My hands fisted in his shirt as I shoved him up against the wall of tools behind him. Frankie gasped in alarm as Noah's eyes widened at me in fear.

"Do not *ever* speak to me about my father or I'll rip your throat out... do ye understand?" I growled, trying to keep the rage at bay. I was one breath from a full shift. If I didn't get my emotions under control, I would go full wolf right where I stood in the barn.

Noah's jaw flexed, but he relented with a solemn nod.

I let him go immediately, heading into the woods to shift without another word to either of them. The moment I was alone in the trees, I broke into a sprint, grateful to hear it was quiet in my mind. There were no other wolves from the pack who were shifted, and I would have my thoughts to myself.

As out of touch with my emotions as I was, I knew I wasn't mad at Noah. I was mad I hadn't Arrowed on Frankie. I was angry beyond belief that she wasn't mine, that I was forbidden from loving the one person on the planet who ever made me feel wholly seen and accepted.

The moment the rage subsided, I began to worry about the consequences of what I'd just done. I had not just attacked one of my few friends, I had threatened the Alpha's son.

It was almost funny. The one action that may have made my old Alpha proud was the one that would likely cause me to lose my new one. I had worked tirelessly to show her my gratitude, to be useful on the ranch, and to convince this new pack to never let me go as my father had. He was my *blood*, and he saw me so easily discarded.

I was nothing to Wolfsblood, and they owed me even less allegiance. Try as I might to be needed, I was still disposable. I was certain the one threat I'd made was more than enough to seal my fate.

I shifted back and re-dressed, ambling out of the woods toward my cabin. As I neared my small home, I saw Noah waiting for me on the steps, and realized he would spare no time delivering my eviction notice.

"I'm sorry," he blurted quickly as I approached, "I shouldn't have mentioned your dad. That was beyond a low blow."

I stopped walking, unsure how to respond. Never before in my life had I gotten an apology after an altercation, let alone one so soon after it had happened. *Was I not going to be exiled again?*

Noah sighed. "You may have noticed, but lately I've developed the unfortunate tendency to act like an ass. It's a terrible habit that I'm trying to kick."

"I'm... truly sorry for how I reacted, too," I replied faintly.

He waved his hand as if my transgressions were already forgotten. "So... you probably know about Chloe," he continued conversationally, shuffling to the right of the step. He tilted his head toward the space he made for me.

Sitting beside him, I tried to appear casual and on board with this change of tone, but my posture remained stiff and alert. "I don't..." I began, unsure what the best response would be.

"Well, you can surmise enough from what Frankie said," Noah continued quickly, "It's true, I started hooking up my best friend. And she's not even a wolf. She's a witch." He looked at me with a wince, anticipating some admonishment.

When I didn't respond again, he hastened to explain, "In my mind, it was just a bit of fun. Just some relief from these strict chains we're shackled in. I wrongly believed that was a mutual understanding, and when her feelings deepened, it all just became so... tragic."

I nodded, and my palm twitched with the question of whether I should place it on his shoulder in comfort. "What you saw with Frankie..." I finally spoke, looking down. I struggled to finish the sentence. *Was I about to reveal the truth of my forbidden desire?*

"I know, man, I know. It was just a hug." Noah dragged his hands down his face with a groan. "I overreacted. I saw you guys and realized I may never be able to hug *my* female best friend like that again. I guess it just hit too close to home. You had every right to call me out."

I shook my head vehemently. "No, I should never have—"

"Dude, *yes*. Please feel free to call me out on my bullshit *anytime*. It's the only way I'll learn." He gave me an encouraging smile.

I was dumbfounded.

"Do you ever wish you had just run away?" Noah wondered

aloud, suddenly feeling museful as he looked up at the sky, "Instead of following your dad's orders to come here, I mean. If you had made a run for it, you could have gotten far enough where you could live a life of your own in your native country."

"I never considered it," I replied honestly.

He sighed. "We can't do *anything* outside the strict confines they put us in. We can't be *anything* other than obedient members of the pack. Sometimes I truly hate it... What is all of this tradition for? It's all pretend. My dad was the strongest wolf I'd ever known and his heart just stopped beating. Like *that.*" He snapped his fingers. "Like he wasn't special... like being a shifter meant *nothing.* We're no better than humans, why do we have to act otherwise?"

This time, I did put a hand on his shoulder.

"What makes all of this worth the trouble?" He turned to look at me.

I took his question seriously, mulling over my thoughts for a moment. "I think," I said slowly, "When we experience the bond, we'll know."

"Maybe you're right about that," Noah acquiesced, "Guess we won't know until it happens... if it *ever* happens." He stood and held a hand to bring me upright as well. "Alright, friend, I've tortured you enough for one night. I'll leave you alone now. But Connall, I hope you know..." He clapped his hands on my shoulders and looked into my eyes with severity. "Despite what your dad may have led you to believe, you don't need a soulmate to be of value here. You're in the land of misfit shifters now. We accept you for all that you are."

Later, as I lay in bed with all the lights on, I replayed our conversation in my head. Initially, I'd found Noah to be irresponsible, abusing his privilege as the Alpha's son to act recklessly. Now, I realized I could relate to him more than I ever would have imagined. Never before had I questioned my duty or my purpose in coming here... until it was clear it would keep me from the one thing in my life I ever dared to want for myself.

CHAPTER 6

Frankie

I paced my bedroom, unable to think about anything other than the feeling of Connall's arms holding me. The way he had wrapped himself around me, it was like being enveloped in the thickest comforter on the coldest night.

Now that I knew the feeling of him, I would be forever left in wanting of his warmth. I'd only meant to thank him, but the moment we collided, it turned into something else.

Neither of us would likely ever admit it to him, but Noah had been right. We had been crossing the line. It wasn't just a hug. It meant so much more because it made me *want* so much more.

I pulled open a dresser drawer and threw the Claddagh ring inside, closing it quickly. I couldn't look at it without feeling as though the butterflies in my stomach were somersaulting.

Was there meaning behind the ring, or did he just give it to me because he thought any 18-year-old girl would appreciate jewelry?

There was a knock on my door, and my heart lurched up into my throat. *Connall?*

"It's Benji." My little brother's high-pitched voice came through the door.

"I said I want to be alone!" I yelled.

"I know!" he bellowed back, "But Mom is making me ask you if it's okay that I have the last piece of your cake!"

"That's fine! Go away!!"

"*Fine!*"

I couldn't stand to be in this house with so many interruptions. A paranoid fear crept in that they could hear what I was thinking, even in human form. Before I allowed myself to second-guess my actions, I opened the window and jumped out, softly landing on the grass below.

Under the cover of the trees, I quickly made my way to my intended destination, my pulse beginning to race out of fear of getting caught. Thankfully, I made the entire journey undetected, and I ran up the steps and knocked promptly on the cabin door.

Almost immediately, Connall opened it.

"What're you doing here so late?" he asked, looking paler than usual. He looked behind me, searching the trees to see if anyone else was with me.

"Aren't you going to invite me in?" I asked. I then coughed, hoping to get some of the embarassing breathiness out of my voice.

"That depends," Connall said slowly, returning his speculative gaze to me.

I rolled my eyes with feigned confidence, pushing past him and entering the small structure. Almost everyone had offered Connall a room in their house, but he had insisted on habituating in one of the lesser-used guest cabins to be of less trouble.

Even now, after living in it for a year, there was no personal décor on the wall, no pictures on the dresser, and nothing to indicate it was a home, apart from the clothes in the closet and the small number of books on the shelf.

It was as if he were still a guest rather than a permanent resident, and my heart ached to think that he truly felt that way.

"Frankie," he said, closing the door after another wary glance outside, "We can't do this. Noah was right. We shouldn't cross any lines."

"I wanted to talk about that."

"I'm sorry I got so upset—"

"Not *that,*" I interrupted, "Noah isn't our Alpha yet. He can't boss us around. You had every right to defend yourself. He has no idea what your life was like in Ireland, or what your dad was like..."

"You do?" he asked, his voice soft.

"You once told me about your brothers. I assume he raised them to be that way. Not to mention the fact that if he could drop you off here, thousands of miles away from your home, and leave in under an hour without so much as a goodbye..."

Connall's eyes fell to the floor, and I regretted the harsh honesty of my words. Almost unconsciously, I moved to hug him again. I had never been much of a touchy-feely person, but I felt in our first embrace that he was not used to receiving affection. I could fix that.

His arms were more immediate this time, enveloping me so rapidly as if they were returning to more a natural position around my torso than they'd been by his side.

"Why are you here?" he asked again, his breath whispering past my ear.

I caught onto the desperation in his tone, and his nose began to caress my neck as he settled himself deeper into our embrace.

"Just between us..." I murmured, my heart starting to race, "I'm not alone in this, am I?"

He took in a sharp breath, slowly moving his hands to my shoulder to gently push me back a full step away from him. "I'm not sure what you mean," he said slowly.

"You're not as good a liar as you think you are," I fibbed. *Or maybe he truly was that obtuse.*

He only stared at me in response, his eyes revealing nothing.

"Okay, well, what if I said I was here to cash in on my birthday wish," I transitioned. His eyebrows raised, and I nervously began to ramble, "I mean, *eighteen* and *never been kissed*... that's kind of sad. Even by shifter standards, don't you think?"

I took a step forward with my pretend pondering, closing the distance once more between us.

"French," he choked on the word.

"*Just one kiss*, Connall," I continued, "It's not breaking the rules, *not really*, and I'll probably be grateful to have some experience under my belt for when my soulmate comes along."

"Frankie. No." His tone shifted from warning to panic, and his eyes were wide with fear as he moved to the door to usher me out.

Immediately, I stopped my pursuit, feeling warm with an onslaught of embarrassment. *Maybe I had gotten it all wrong, after all.*

"Oh, well. Worth a shot," I sang, trying to hold tight to my last bit of dignity as I moved to leave. I couldn't stop myself from throwing out some petty parting words as I passed him, "I'll go see if Milo's up for it."

His hand shot and gripped my upper arm, halting me. For a moment, I thought he was going to start another *noble* lecture about not crossing the line... until I saw the expression on his face:

He looked ravenous.

He pulled me back to him, his other hand moving to the back of my neck as he crashed his lips onto mine. My heart leaped into my throat, preventing me from emitting any noise of surprise. The only sound I could hear was the harsh inhale of his breath through his nose and my heart hammering in my ears as the fullness of his lips pressed against me. When he pulled back by an inch, and our kiss broke, I opened my eyes, already grieving the moment was over.

But it wasn't over, because as I leaned away further and he met the half-lidded plea in my gaze, he dipped his head and began kissing me once more. This time, I couldn't *not* make a sound. I moaned in reply, enraptured by the novel sensation of lips moving against mine, *Connall's* lips moving against mine. My hands haphazardly dragged their way around his stomach, his chest, his shoulders— everywhere I always longed to explore. He was growing just as frantic as I was, his hands moving to grip my hips, pulling me up tightly against him with a gravelly rumble in his throat.

He then moved a hand to my hair, embedding a fist at the nape, and gently forced my head to tilt to the side. The moment my throat was exposed, he moved his kisses to devour the crook of my neck, nipping and sucking at the sensitive skin.

I nearly melted into the floor, my knees wobbling from the fire stoked within me. With newfound fervor, I pulled his face back to mine, our kisses increasingly chaotic and frenzied, but *my God,* was it the greatest thing I'd ever experienced—

—until I was pushed out of his door onto the front steps, hearing the door slam and lock behind me.

"Go home, Frankie!" he yelled through the wood.

It took a second for my soul to return to my body, and I stood there in shock, the chill of the air seeping into the heat of my skin. I glared at the door, throwing my hands up in frustration. "*What the fuck?*"

He flicked off the porch light, sending the message loud and clear.

I wanted to scream more obscenities. Instead, I held up a middle finger and stormed away.

As I walked back to mine, bitter tears began clouding my eyes. He had given me every indication he was enjoying what was happening, only to throw me out in the next second? *And on my birthday, no less!*

My arms crossed tightly to brace myself against the chill of the air. Apparently, I had been in such a hurry to embarrass myself that I hadn't thought to put a coat on before I left my house. The cold I could manage with the body heat I had as a shifter, but the sting of the wind against my skin was irritating.

He threw me outside in the cold, I thought bitterly, clinging to my anger. I may have been distracted heading over, but on the return, I could not deny the feeling that I *hated* walking the ranch alone at night. I usually forced Benji to walk with me or came up with some random excuse to head home before sundown. It just always felt creepy, ever since...

"Hello, little pup," he had said, seemingly coming out of nowhere.

I winced at the sight of him. I was young and easily frightened and I had to remind myself he was my uncle's— the Alpha's— friend. He wouldn't hurt me.

"B-Beau," I stuttered his name. He had become, without a doubt, the most feared member of our pack— always so unpredictable. Even though he was smiling at me, my shoulders were braced for one of his violent mood swings.

"What are you doing out so late?" he asked me, striding closer, "Isn't it past your bedtime?"

"I was watching a movie at Noah's," I explained quickly, "My parents know I'm coming home now. They're probably waiting for me on the porch." It was a lie and a bad one at that. I just felt the need to let him know people were expecting me.

"Well, then, I'll walk you," he offered, holding out a hand.

I weakly took it, and we started walking much slower than I wanted. I cringed in the silence between us until I noticed his other arm was carrying what looked to be a bulky leather book.

"What's that?" I asked, my curiosity getting the better of me.

The way he smiled in response, I wish I hadn't asked.

"It's a very special book," he sneered, "The words inside do magical things. Would you like me to read something to you?"

"That's okay," I said lightly, "I just want to get home."

"It can make wishes come true," he sang teasingly, "It's going to make all my wishes come true."

"That's okay," I repeated more firmly, sliding my hand from his. "Actually, I think I'm in the mood to run home."

"Smart little pup," he complimented. "Go ahead. *Run.*"

The moment I heard the growl behind the final word, I did as he commanded and took off, resisting the urge to look back and see if he was chasing me. The more I ran, the more I felt myself grow angry. I wanted to turn around and scream and yell at him for trying to scare me. I wanted to scream at myself for letting him get away with it. He was always playing sick pranks to scare the younger members of the pack. It was high time someone stood up against him for it.

But I said nothing and continued running until I was in my bedroom, the door locked.

That was the last time I interacted directly with Beau. The tragic string of events in our pack began some time thereafter, and each misfortune spurned him further into madness. When Uncle Killian passed, he finally broke down completely. He ran away, somewhere far from where Adeline could call him back, and we never heard from him again.

The pack was happy to move on from Beau, and rarely was his name mentioned. Though he no longer infected our days, I knew I would never forget that night or the way he'd said, *"Run."*

At the memory of his voice, I broke into a full sprint toward the safety of my home. With every stride, I felt myself grow increasingly angry as I had on that night. Only I wasn't thinking of our creepy ex-pack member. I was thinking of smashing every acoustic record in my room, cutting my hair short, and burning the shirt Connall once said brought out the color of my eyes. I was thinking that I would *never* be tossed out like that again, and I was thinking that if I could not love him, then I would forevermore *hate Connall O'Faolain.*

PART THREE

The Third Year

CHAPTER 7

Connall

I walked into the classroom for my final class of the day, Environmental Science 150, and my spine immediately straightened at the sight of Frankie. She was dressed in her usual black t-shirt and sat alone at one of the lab tables, bent over a notebook. As I surveyed the rest of the room, I realized the seat next to hers was the only one open.

I knew why no one had chosen her as a lab partner. Most people were drawn to her beauty, but she always demanded to be left alone. Word traveled fast through the small college, and eventually, the entire campus body shut her out completely.

I couldn't ever manage to do the same. Since I kissed her on her birthday, it was like Frankie had banished me to the center of a frozen lake, putting a vast and icy distance between us. Despite her glares and all the insults she threw at me, I still found myself quietly following her around the ranch at a distance like a lost donkey, hoping someday she'd accept my company again.

"Please take your seat, sir," the professor said, pulling me from my trance.

My neck warmed as I moved to the open chair.

Frankie never lifted her head from her notebook, but I could tell from the way she stiffened in her seat that she knew I was there.

"You haven't gotten your science credit out of the way yet?" she muttered through clenched teeth.

"I'm afraid not," I murmured back.

"Well then," she said with a sigh, "Just my fucking luck."

I stared down at the table, trying not to let her words sting. I was confounded by the depth of her hatred for me. After replaying that night over in my mind a million times, I still believed she'd *wanted* me to kiss her. She had even called it her *birthday wish.*

Yet, from the moment it happened, her words in and out of wolf form declared to all that she *despised me* and wanted nothing to do with me.

"What did you do?" Noah once asked me after he caught on to the vitriol in her mind. "I mean, I've wondered on occasion if I've pissed off Frankie past the point of no return, but this is a whole new level of grudge for her."

"Your guess is as good as mine," I replied forlornly.

The feeling of her lips on mine and the taste of her skin consumed every dream, every night. It had been the brightest moment of my life, followed by the darkest. It was one form of damnation to want her, but another hell entirely to have had her in my arms for just a moment and then lose her completely.

She continued to distractedly scribble in her notebook, and I couldn't help myself from engaging with her once more. When it came to her, I was either afflicted with a poor memory or masochism. It was as though I always had to lift the lid of the basket *one more time* to check if the viper inside would bite.

"What are you drawing?" I murmured, lowering my voice to a volume the professor wouldn't hear as he began the class.

She tried to hide it, but I caught sight of it anyway: a near-perfect sketch of a wolf. It was not someone I recognized.

"Who is that?"

"No one. I'm just doodling to pass the time."

"That's more than a doodle."

"What were you expecting me to be mindlessly scribbling? 'Mrs. O'Faolain?'"

She was probably aiming for a dig, but I enjoyed hearing her refer to herself as my Mrs. far too much for her intended offense to take any effect.

"I didn't know you could draw," I commented, "I should've bought you a sketchbook instead of that ring."

She spoke through her teeth with her increasing frustration, "What?"

"The gold ring I gave you for your birthday last year. You never wear it." We were in dangerous territory, discussing her birthday, but I had to know what happened to it.

"I hate gold. I threw it away." She flipped to a new page, tuning into the professor and taking notes.

Yep, the viper bites, I thought miserably. I turned away as my hopes plummeted, pretending to focus my attention ahead. We did not speak for the rest of the class.

When the lecture ended, we walked in silence together to meet the others at the front of campus. I was surprised Frankie even permitted me to walk alongside her, and it took the whole trip for me to come up with something to say. Just as I opened my mouth, however, Frankie ran ahead to sneak up behind Noah. He was staring at a couple sharing an ice cream and didn't see her until she'd knocked his stack of books out of his hand.

"Real mature, Frankie," he muttered, immediately moving to pick them up.

"What's your dad making for dinner tonight, Milo?" Frankie asked, ignoring Noah.

Milo shook his head. "My dad said there won't be access to the kitchen tonight. There's a private event that will go pretty late."

My shoulders dropped slightly. The days I didn't have access to the Main Building's kitchen were the days I ate microwaved meals.

It was all the kitchenette in my small cabin offered. Secretly, I loved to cook, and I missed having access to a stove and oven, but I couldn't dare impose on anyone's property.

"What if we made our *own* dinner?" Frankie asked, "We could go to Wilsons and pick up some things. Your mom has the best kitchen, Noah, but we could also use mine..."

"That could be fun!" As with most plans, Milo was immediately on board. "What is everyone in the mood for?"

"I vote for tacos," Noah said, "Ma probably won't trust us with anything too intricate."

"We eat that every week. Can you cook, Connall?" Frankie asked. Suddenly, her bright green eyes were on me and I found it hard to breathe under the direct eye contact I had not been graced with in so long.

"Aye— I mean, yes," I stammered, "But traditional Irish stuff. Nothing you guys would enjoy."

"Hey, I *love* Irish food," Noah protested.

"If you're down to cook, I'm down to eat," Milo said with a smile.

"Sounds like a plan," Frankie declared.

⋙——◇——⋘

Several hours later, we were all sitting in front of a freshly devoured, hearty meal. Just taking in the scent of my favorite recipes from home brought a bittersweet weight in my gut.

"Here's a fun game!" Milo clapped his hands together. "Let's go around the table... describe what you think your soulmate looks like."

"If I knew she existed, I wouldn't be here," Noah spoke as he finished his second serving, "I'd be out there looking for her."

Milo laughed and mimed holding up a flyer. *"'Have you seen this person? Neither have I, just hoping to meet her!'"*

"Frankie could sketch the portrait for you," I murmured.

"What? You draw?" Noah asked, turning to his cousin in surprise. "How come I didn't know that?"

"I don't *draw*, I doodle, and not very well," she dismissed, "Anyway, what do you mean, *'if she existed?'*"

"Oh, come on," he groaned, shifting in his seat as he looked around at everyone. "Sooner or later, we have to accept that the bond isn't going to happen for us. Do you really think *all* of the eligibles in the pack *just haven't met the right one* yet?"

I was silent, moving the last of my cabbage around my plate. Noah was naturally cynical surrounding the matters of our kind, but he had a point. Other packs had Arrows occur all the time, and yet Wolfsblood had remained stagnant in its numbers for *years*. For me, it then begged the question:

If it was highly likely that the soulmate bond would never happen for us... why did we need to wait for it?

"Do we think Connall's mate likes long hair?" Milo asked, blatantly ignoring Noah's skepticism. He leaned over and playfully swatted the ends of my hair off the edge of my shoulder.

"It's an interesting look, that's for sure," Frankie mumbled, her voice barely audible.

Immediately, I became defensive, pulling it up into a haphazard bun with the elastic on my wrist. "I don't know how to cut my hair."

"Neither do I. That's why I go to the barber in town," Noah spoke as if it were obvious.

"I can't drive."

The table was silent, and everyone slowly turned to look at me with surprise in their eyes. It had suddenly dawned on them why I rarely left the ranch, apart from our shared carpools to class. I never wanted to be a nuisance and ask for a ride anywhere else.

My neck warmed with embarrassment. "It's alright—"

"No, it's not. We should've covered that years ago with the other paperwork," Noah insisted, his hand fisting on the table.

"I can help you get the hours of practice for a license," Milo offered immediately.

"I can cut your hair," Frankie added. This time, the table turned to look at *her* in surprise, and she squirmed in her seat. "If you want," she added weakly. She glared at Noah and Milo with full ferocity. *"What?!"*

"You draw, you cut hair, what other secrets are you hiding?" Noah teased.

"You also don't make your lack of... *friendliness* toward Connall a secret," Milo said with a gentle smile, "We just think it's *mighty sweet* of you to help, Frances."

"Shut up," she scoffed, "He made us dinner. I can even the score and cut his hair, just so I don't owe him anything."

"Speaking of this *delicious* meal, I don't think I can eat another bite." Milo leaned back in his chair and patted his stomach.

"Then don't," Frankie said, "Connall worked hard. He deserves to have some leftovers."

I was shaken by these sudden acts of kindness from her. *Was she genuinely looking out for me, or was it just a show of keeping the peace for her friends?*

I had to know. Later, as we gathered our things to head out, I murmured to her privately. "Can I walk you home?"

"I suppose that'd be okay," she answered slowly, "Not to say that I need a chaperone, but I really hate walking alone at night."

CHAPTER 8

Frankie

I thought maybe he wanted to talk, but we walked in the same awkward silence as we had after class. His first words to me weren't until I almost reached my front door:

"Why did you suggest I cook tonight?"

"I don't know." His steady gaze was unforthcoming, and I found myself beginning to ramble, "Maybe I'm just tired of tacos and wanted something different. I once heard you talking to Nathan about helping him in the kitchen for St. Patrick's Day. Figured your cooking would be better than anything Noah could come up with."

From the twitching of the corners of his lips, I could tell he could read through my bullshit. He knew I asked him to cook because I cared.

Silence fell between us again and I deflated.

"I didn't throw the ring away, okay?" I admitted, giving up the ruse. It was a cruel lie, and I'd spent the rest of the dayin regret, trying to make up for it. "It's in my drawer upstairs."

"I'm glad to hear it," he said matter-of-factly, "It was my mother's."

The weight of that admission hung in the air between us, those four words dissipating any bitterness I had been holding onto so tightly in the last year.

"Connall," I whispered, tears suddenly brimming my eyes. *How could he give away something so precious to him?* Unconsciously, I moved a hand to lay over my chest, my heart aching for him.

His eyes flicked down to my hand and back up to my eyes.

"As ucht Dé," he murmured, his brogue thick. He dropped the leftovers from his arms, and before I could react, his hands were on my waist, pushing me backward until I was up against the side of the house, enveloped in the shadows.

"What are you doing?" I whispered in a panic. *Was this really happening again? Now? What if somebody saw us?*

He took another small step forward, his hands still on my waist and his fingers gripping me harshly. He was breathing heavily, his brows furrowed and his eyes suddenly full of all the emotions he buried as he silently implored me for a sign to keep going.

Despite all the thoughts eddying my mind, I managed to give him an almost imperceptible nod.

He inhaled sharply and pulled me up against him, closing any distance between us and claiming my mouth with his. This kiss was much different from the last one—it was a firm, steady, unfrenzied possession of my lips.

I couldn't tell which kind I liked more, and I wondered if I'd need one more taste of the frenzy to determine for certain. With a growing hunger, I moved my lips against his, my mouth opening as my fingers embedded themselves in his long hair. He pulled back a few inches, and my lips unconsciously moved to chase his, but he laid a hand on my chest, holding me still.

"Let's just do it," he whispered, his hand moving to the back of my neck as he leaned his forehead against mine.

"Do what?" I asked, my brain full of static.

"Be together, French."

Hearing the nickname he hadn't used in so long, I stilled, crashing back to Earth. "But... you said... we can't—"

"We *can,*" he disagreed restlessly, "We can."

"We *can't* because... we didn't Arrow." Never had I been able to admit it out loud before. Tears were flowing down my face now, and in a moment of heartbreaking intimacy, he brushed them away with his thumbs as he held my face in earnest.

"I don't care," he swore to me, his ardent gaze turning distraught, "We can lie or we can run away. *I don't care.* I just... want this."

It felt like the ground was going to move out from underneath me.

"Do you, French?"

Like the motorbike crash when I was 17, I was barreling out of control, my skin aflame. "I— ah— what?"

He buried his head in my neck, running his nose from my clavicle to my ear with a guttural groan. The butterflies in my stomach somersaulted at the sound of it. "This is agony," he rasped, "I can't stand another day of this... *desperately* wanting you. Tell me now, do you want this too? Do you want me?"

"Connall," I begged. *I just needed a second... some air, some time to think!*

"French." His tone was a warning.

"I do want you..." I admitted. He crashed into me again, wrapping his arms around my waist to squeeze me tightly as the rest of my words spilled out, "But not like this."

My answer surprised us both.

He froze and slowly unfurled himself from me, his gaze darkening. He turned to pick up his discarded tupperware, suddenly furious when he straightened. "Are you— *How can you*— Just what are you doing to me?!"

I let out a surprised chortle at the question. "What am *I* doing—"

"Yes, Frankie, exactly what are you doing to me?" he demanded, "From the moment I arrived here, have I just been some toy to you? Something to play with until you get bored?"

"Excuse me?!"

"You came to my cabin!" He was yelling, apparently not giving a damn who heard, "You asked me to kiss you!"

"And you threw me out!" I yelled back. "You told me to go home!" *If anyone was acting hot and cold, it was him!*

"BECAUSE IF I HADN'T STOPPED IT, I WOULD'VE—" He cut himself off, throwing his head back to release an angry roar. When his head fell back down, he was panting harder, the growl of an oncoming rage-shift clouding his breath.

"Breathe, Connall, breathe." I stepped forward, placing my hand on his chest to calm him.

He looked at me with such anger in his eyes that I immediately dropped my hand.

"I don't understand you," I said, my voice breaking, *"You* pushed *me* away. *You* told me we couldn't cross the line. I've hated you since then because you never even tried to talk about it with me or apologize for throwing me out! What changed?!"

"I've already said I don't care about that cursed line," he snarled through his teeth, "My father be damned, for all I care—"

I gasped. "Is that what this is? Revenge against your dad?" I blurted the accusation the moment it occurred to me, "You might want me now when you're feeling vengeful, Connall, but what will happen when your conscience kicks in?"

His fists curled at his side as he spoke through his teeth, "My dad has *nothing* to do with this!"

"I think he has everything to do with this." I disagreed. *If I had been exiled by my father, I would want to spite him just the same.* "If you think for the second time I'm going to cross a line with you, only to be thrown aside the moment you feel guilty, then you can go straight to hell." I turned away from him and stormed into my house.

Just before the door closed behind me, I thought I heard him say, "How can I, when I'm already there?"

I sighed. Maybe I *was* just a way for Connall to get back at his dad. He was no better than Noah, rebelling against the rules the Alphas put in place, but he was too good, too honorable to act disobedient for long. If I had agreed to be with him, he would have surely discarded me the moment his guilt caught up to him.

I moved to the staircase, intending to run to my room to cry in private when I took notice of my little brother in his space-print pajamas in the living room. He was kneeling toward the back of the couch, his eyes set outside the window.

He'd seen and heard everything.

"Oh, for Pete's sake, Benji." I groaned.

"You guys kissed?" he whispered, turning to look at me from over his shoulder.

"It didn't mean anything!" I insisted, "We didn't do anything wrong. So, you don't need to tell mom and dad."

"I wouldn't tell them!" he promised, "I'm not a snitch."

"Good. Thanks." The panic that was raging in my gut subsided. I turned to leave, but my brother spoke up once more.

"I think you guys are perfect for each other."

"Except in the one and only way that counts," I replied sadly.

Three days passed, and I managed to evade Connall everywhere except for my dreams. I didn't know what to say to him or how we could get past our kiss this time. As badly as I wanted to just go back to pretending to hate him, too much had happened.

I'd shown my cards, and he'd shown his, but still, nothing could come from it. We just had to walk away from the table.

I spent a lot of my time in the barn, essentially just banging my wrench against anything that would make a noise loud enough to dull the frustrations that screamed in my head. I kept getting phantom sensations of his lips on mine or how my hand felt moving through his hair.

The moment the thought entered my mind, I felt it once more, those red waves gliding between my fingers—

I threw the wrench across the room as if it could take my memories with it.

"Well, darn," Benji said casually from the entryway. "I was coming to invite you to play catch with us, but it seems like you're already pitching in a dangerous game of your own."

I winced and turned to see my brother standing beside Connall, who was unsurprisingly blank-eyed and stony-faced.

"I told him you were probably busy," Connall said softly, his tone just as stagnant as his expression.

I could always rely on family to arrange a deeply embarrassing moment for me. "You... you guys are playing catch?" I asked breathlessly.

"Only for the past hour," Benji said with a wide smile, "But it's getting kind of boring just the two of us. You wanna join?"

I looked down, cracking my knuckles to keep from showing too much emotion. *How many times had Benji begged one of the guys to play with him?* Even when they did oblige him, Milo or Noah only entertained him for about ten minutes at the most before they got bored. And here was Connall, after everything that had just transpired, throwing the ball with my little brother for *a full hour.*

"I have a better idea for a game," I said, tucking my hands into the back pockets of my denim shorts. "We're going to play Barbershop."

"What's that?" my brother asked excitedly.

"We pretend we're in a barbershop and cut Connall's hair," I explained, forcing myself to meet Connall's eyes with meaning. I still wanted to follow through on my promise, and hoped it might be less awkward if Benji was there to act as a buffer.

"I'll pass," Benji said lightly, ruining my plan, "But don't stop the game on my account! Have fun!" Without another word, he broke into a full sprint away from us.

My eyes narrowed. *What was he up to?* "Bring me a comb and Dad's clippers!" I yelled after him.

Connall moved to me, dropping his voice to a murmur. "You really don't have to—"

Evading his touch, I dragged a wheeled stool to the dirty sink we only used to wash the grease off our hands. "Welcome. Please have a seat, sir."

He eyed me warily before he obliged, his posture straight in alarm even as he sat.

"You can relax. I promise I won't waterboard you." I pushed his shoulders to lean backward. Holding my breath, I removed the elastic that held half his hair up, emptied the full length of his hair into the sink, and started the faucet. "Is the temperature to your liking?" I asked softly as I relished in the feeling of his long red waves sliding through my fingers once more.

"It's a little cold," he admitted with a squint.

"Too bad, that's the only temperature we got."

A rumble echoed in his chest, and I found myself sufficiently distracted by the sheer victory of having made Connall laugh.

If only Noah and Milo had been here to witness it. Then again, as I bent closer to the sink and felt Connall's hand move to my leg to brush his thumb against the side of my knee, I was sincerely relieved they weren't anywhere close by.

He must've heard my breath hitch because as soon as his hand was there, it was gone. "Sorry," he murmured, closing his eyes in regret.

"It's okay," I replied, my throat thick, "I know you have a— how did you phrase it? *A high affinity for my legs.*"

He laughed once more. "You remember that, huh? That's unfortunate. It wasn't my finest moment." We were silent for a short while, until he spoke once more, his voice barely above a murmur, "For the record, I have a high affinity for every part of you."

"Likewise," I whispered the confession. I cut the water and passed him one of our cleaner towels, one that only had a *little* bit of grease.

"Is that right? You even like the shaggy hair?" he asked as he tilted his head and wrung out the extra water.

"It's why I offered to cut it," I answered, crossing my arms with a smirk. "It would be... easier for me not to see you rock that ridiculously sexy man-bun that you do all the time."

His eyes widened, and only then did I realize that I had just called him *sexy*. My chest flushed with embarrassment as I looked away with an awkward cough.

He was suddenly leaning forward, and his large hand wrapped around my wrist to pull me to him. I collided with him clumsily, falling directly into his lap with a loud gasp. The moment I felt the breadth of his chest under my hands, my body moved on its own accord. Desperately, I hitched my legs to either side of him, my fingers curling over the dense muscles of his shoulders as one of his hands wrapped itself around my thigh and the other moved into my hair. His long fingers drew in fist around my curls, bringing my face closer to his with a gravelly rumble in his throat.

"French," he groaned, brushing his nose along the side of mine.

I could only release a quiet whimper in reply. My skin was humming, my ears ringing, and the warmth that pooled in my lower abdomen told me that, to my very core, I craved far more than just another brief kiss from Connall. I couldn't stand for anything less than being *consumed by him*.

"I got the clippers!" I heard my brother yell from some distance away.

Connall cursed as I released a panicked squeal and threw myself backward, crashing to the ground in my scramble to put as much distance between him and me before my little brother returned. I cleared my throat, dusting my ass off as I stood. "That can never happen again," I said quickly, "Benji can't—"

"Just between us," Connall affirmed, repeating our old saying as he straightened his posture and cleared his throat, "And... I'll keep my hair short. To make things easier."

I swallowed with a nod. "I can wear snow pants year round."

He smiled, and I nearly stumbled backward once more at the sight of it. "Nah, you needn't worry about me. *I* can control myself."

I snorted at his sarcasm, and moved to the barn entrance to greet my brother. The moment I turned away from Connall, I fought an unexpected onslaught of tears. In some ways, it felt good to have things out in the open. In others, it felt painfully tragic to be making jokes about our intense attraction to one another, knowing we would likely never act on it again.

CHAPTER 9

Frankie

The downpour of rain hitting the roof of the barn almost drowned out my music as I secretly worked on replacing the tire of an ATV. Benji had gone for a secret little joy ride and accidentally popped the back wheel. Given his choice to protect my secrets over the last year, I had promised to fix the error without telling on him.

I moved to grab a new tire off the wall, feeling Connall's quiet arrival before I saw it with my eyes. With a smile, I turned to greet him, only to see this would be one of the times we weren't alone.

"What happened here?" Milo asked, peering over the side of the ATV.

"Someone popped a tire," I answered vaguely.

"Someone?" Milo pressed.

I glared at him, a warning not to push it further.

Milo grinned in response, his teeth a bright white against his tanned skin. He rarely took my threatening looks seriously. "So... Summit's coming up. Wanna take bets on who will Arrow? My money's on Connall."

"He didn't Arrow last time and it's the same people," I rejected the thought immediately. I couldn't imagine how I would react if Connall found his soulmate in front of me, and I'd been dreading the mass congregation of shifters since we'd received the invitation to Mexico.

"Maybe someone new has come of age," Milo continued, turning from me to Connall, who was looking paler than usual. "Do you think you could be into someone a tiny bit younger, Con?"

I looked away from them, feeling myself blush furiously at the question while Milo obliviously laughed at Connall's silence.

"Not sure what *two blinks* mean in morse code, but I'm guessing it's no," Milo continued, "I'm just teasing, man. If anyone's going to Arrow, it'll be—"

"Me," I finished, turning back around.

Milo's eyebrows raised with entertained surprise. "Confident, are you?"

"It's going to be me," I said definitively, "I was too young at the last Summit. This time will be different. I'm going to strut through those beach resort doors, find my soulmate, and leave this pile of horse shit behind forever."

Milo's laughter was cut off when Connall stood suddenly, walking off into the rain with his fists balled at his side. We watched him depart, an inquisitive frown growing on Milo's face.

"The Arrow is a sensitive subject when it comes to the Summit," I reminded us both with a sigh. "He's going to be seeing his family there, and they're going to discover he hasn't done the one thing he was unfairly sent here to do."

"Shit, you're right! I should've been more mindful of that," he replied, regret in his tone. "I'll go apologize."

"Let me," I said, holding out a hand, "I'm the one who bragged it was going to happen for me." I took a deep breath before I headed out into the rain. Thick droplets from the torrential downpour pelted my face and made it nearly impossible for me to see.

I thought maybe Connall would be walking back to his cabin, but something in my gut told me he had headed in the other direction... toward the woods.

In the middle of a rainstorm?

I almost doubted the instinct, but, sure enough, I found him standing by the forest edge. He was bent over, leaning his hands on a tree and panting.

As I got closer, I saw the damage he had done. In a matter of seconds, he had punched the thin tree so harshly that he nearly splintered the trunk in half. Despite the rain sluicing down his arms, some blood remained on his healing knuckles.

"Con!" I yelled, running over, "Are you okay?"

He looked up at me, intense rage in his eyes. "If you've come to gloat some more about finding your soulmate, *I won't be hearin' it.*"

"I'm sorry," I said, stepping closer than I usually dared so that I didn't have to yell over the rain, "I shouldn't have said that. I was just playing along."

He blinked repeatedly, just staring at me as some unspoken thoughts swirled behind his stony exterior.

"It won't happen for any of us," I tried to assure him.

He shook his head. "You were right; last time, you were too young. This time..."

I recognized the dread in his tone— the same dread I felt when I thought about him finding his mate. I eyed the damage to the tree and then returned my eyes to him, seeing the truth: *He wasn't just upset about disappointing his father. He was upset at the prospect of losing me.*

"Connall," I whispered, my heart breaking. I took one final step forward, taking his hand in mine to examine his knuckles more closely as the rain washed away the blood that remained. I closed my eyes, trying not to cry from the pain aching in my chest.

He leaned his forehead against mine, slowly shaking his head once more. "I'm sorry," he muttered, but I wasn't sure what he was apologizing for.

I raised his knuckles to my lips, brushing a chaste kiss across the wounds that had already healed. Despite the downpour of rain around us, I heard his sharp intake of breath. He moved his hand to cup my jaw, his thumb flashing across my bottom lips as he lifted my chin to look at him, his gaze heated.

"French," he said softly, his tone thick with some unreadable emotion. *A warning? A plea?*

"Maybe it would be for the best," I offered weakly, leaning into the embrace of his palm, "If I did Arrow at the Summit. If I left, you could be free of this torture. Just one look, and you wouldn't—"

A murderous growl released from his throat, and he gripped my arms firmly, moving me so that I was clear out of the way just before he rage-shifted.

The moment he was a wolf, he took off into the forest, sprinting far away from me.

His reaction confirmed it. At the Summit, I needed to Arrow, and I needed to find my soulmate to eradicate the despair I felt watching him disappear into the darkness of the trees.

I kept thinking about it throughout a restless night and into the early morning that followed. It was always an unanswered question between us: *why* we hadn't Arrowed when we felt so pulled to one another.

Was it because we didn't have someone else destined for us?

If one of us Arrowed on another wolf, we would know, without a semblance of a doubt, that there could never be anything more between us. Selfishly, I hoped it was me who got to move on from this misery I felt. As I began to picture Connall, his arms around some other woman—

It made me want to do *far worse* than run my fist through a tree.

In a rage, I flung the covers off my bed and climbed out the window. The moment my feet landed in the dewy grass, I broke out into a sprint toward his cabin.

He opened the door on my third round of knocking.

"Just so you know," I held up a hand before he questioned my intrusion at such an ungodly hour, "If you *do* meet your soulmate at the Summit, I will probably want to kill her."

It was silent, my words hanging in the misty morning air.

"At least at first." I amended weakly.

He leaned against the doorframe, his pale biceps naturally flexing as he crossed his arms. "Good to know."

My eyes fell to his arms, and I had to bite my lip to keep from licking it with hunger. The sight of his bare chest and arms always did something to me.

"Yeah, so, um, just keep that in mind, okay?" I finished breathlessly. I lifted my stare from his chest to his eyes... only to find *his* gaze was focused on *my* chest as well.

I realized then that despite the chilly morning air, I was only wearing a thin tank top and pajama pants. Taking in his heady stare, I felt a familiar and treasonous warmth pool in my lower abdomen. Everywhere else, I felt cold.

The others would be getting up soon. I couldn't be caught out in the woods dressed like this. Why didn't I just text this to him? Why did my impulsions always bring me to his doorstep?!

As if hearing the question in my mind, Connall's eyes snapped up to mine, awakening from his dazed stupor with a guilty expression.

Sensing his regret, I winced. "Well. Good talk." I started to turn away when I felt his warm hand against my arm, his fingers curling around me swiftly in the same way he stopped me from leaving on my birthday.

With a gasp, I turned back around to face him, my body closing the distance before my mind could catch up and tell me it was wrong. His other hand flashed out quickly to hold me still, not pushing me away nor pulling me in. My palm hovered over his chest as his gaze drifted down to my mouth with an unspoken question before returning to search my eyes for the answer in a tantalizing, triangular motion.

Whatever he saw in my face was answer enough.

Delicately, he dipped his head lower to mine. As I held my breath and tilted my face upward, closing the distance between us even further, the morning light broke through the trees and enveloped us in its brilliance, shattering the allure of the shadows we'd been in.

We became still as we read each other's half-lidded gaze, daring the other one to make the bold move in broad daylight.

But neither of us would.

"Wait here," he said softly after a moment, his mouth hovering less than an inch from mine. "I'll walk you back."

I remained frozen with my palm still raised as he broke his hold on me and disappeared inside his home. The moment he stepped into his cabin, I came back to life and hugged my arms around myself, wishing it was him who could hold me freely in the sunlight.

I dropped my arms when he came back out, thankfully with a T-shirt on. With a tilt of his head, he gestured for us to walk.

"That's not necessary, Con," I said quickly, though I moved to follow. "You should just go back to bed."

"You don't like walking alone when it's dark, and the sun is only just rising," he replied simply.

I looked back at the treacherous light that glowed through the trees, suddenly wishing for the first time it remained dark. "It's only the middle of the night that I— wait, how do you know that?" As a rule, I didn't make a habit of declaring my weaknesses.

He looked over at me, a solitary brow furrowing as if it was obvious. "You told me last year."

My lips parted in surprise at how easily I revealed secret parts of myself to him. We were silent for a while, our pace slow and unhurried as we took in the sound of the natural world around us waking up.

"If *I* don't meet my soulmate at the Summit," he said softly, "And *you* don't meet *yours...*"

"Then we'll run away together and join the circus?" I joked. The moment the words left my mouth, I regretted them.

The corner of his lips lifted slightly. "And here I was thinking you *hated* Milo's trapeze."

I sighed softly with the relief that he was humoring me. "I wouldn't be an aerialist," I argued, "I'd be the lion tamer."

"And what role am I to play? The lion?"

"Are you kidding?" Without thinking, I laid a hand on his bicep. "Strong Man, *obviously.*"

He stopped walking, his eyes drifting down to my hand, which had not moved yet from his arm. I yanked it away, hugging myself once more as I strode ahead.

"The circus is our only option?" he asked as he caught up to my strides. "We can't run away and be... *tax accountants* together?"

The question hit me like a ton of bricks. "No," I affirmed, my voice barely above a whisper. "We *can't.*"

"Guess I'll have to grow a mustache then," he murmured, but there was no more humor in his tone.

"Buy a unitard while you're at it."

"No need. I have plenty already."

I threw my head back and laughed almost too loudly. Connall so rarely showed his playful side. Even after so many years of egging him on, hearing him crack a joke was still a thrilling surprise.

We said nothing more to each other until just before we arrived at my house.

"Thanks for walking with me," I said lamely, uncertain where we were leaving things.

"I'll always walk you through the darkness, French," he said, "You needn't even ask." Without another word, he turned and walked away from me.

I stared after him, my chest aching as he disappeared into the light of the sunrise. When I moved to go inside, my resolve was firm. We couldn't keep hurting each other like this. One of us had to put an end to it once and for all.

One of us had to Arrow.

CHAPTER 10

Connall

I moved to the table of refreshments, avoiding the eyes of everyone I passed. Frankie, on the contrary, had been desperate to connect eyes with every wolf on the grounds of the Mexican pack's resort.

I'd thought we'd reached an understanding back at Wolfsblood. The moment we arrived here, however, she changed her tune, dangling her frantic search for a mate right in front of my eyes. Especially at this formal dance held for the unbonded, Frankie took up every wolf on their offer for a dance. I couldn't stand to see everyone's hunger for her, resenting how it mirrored my own. The moment I'd seen her in the hallway in a red dress that hugged every curve, it was all I could do not to reach out and run my hands over her silhouette. As badly as I wanted to be the partner that twirled her around the room, I couldn't risk what I would do in the proximity to her staggering beauty.

I found Noah stood by a table, a plate of food in his hand as he awkwardly bobbed his head along to the music, and I moved to stand next to him.

"Any luck?" he murmured, leaning over to me.

I gave him a look, not even bothering to shake my head.

"This is ridiculous!" He let out a frustrated laugh, "The way they parade us in front of each other and try to force it to happen. We might as well just go down the line in a staring contest. Besides, if a couple *were* to Arrow, the last thing they would wanna do after *that* is a waltz."

My mouth ran dry. I couldn't think about Frankie and her soulmate... the mating frenzy that occurred when the bond locked into place. Some bonded wolves didn't resurface for *days*.

"Never thought Frankie would be so eager, either." Noah continued, "I think this is the most prim and pleasant I've seen her. There's no way these wolves are falling for that sweetheart act."

"It sure looks like they are." I grimaced at the sight of her grinning as she was spun in a circle. The skirt of her dress fanned out with the movement, and her curls that had broken free from her intricate updo flounced around her face. As she twirled back toward her partner, I felt pulled in closer, like she was a hurricane and I was feeble against her centrifugal force. "Shall we go elsewhere?" I asked, tearing my eyes away.

Noah nodded, swallowing his hors d'oeuvre. "Please. Angel and Cody from the Idaho pack are lurking around here somewhere. They said they had some kind of party drug. Might be funny to watch them act like idiots."

His words triggered a memory:

'Do you want some?' he asked. My eyes moved down to the pipe in his hand, the smoke rising from it smelled of plum and truffle.

Frankie's laughter broke through the vision, and my eyes followed the joyful sound. My pleasure dissipated the moment I saw the cause. Two younger boys were pushing each other, almost fighting to have the next turn at a dance with her.

I tore my gaze away again. "Let's go."

We left the ballroom and quietly made our way down the hallway. We knew if Adeline were to catch on that we'd left, she would send Noah right back in there and force him to dance with somebody. I was more of a free agent, but I still didn't want to disappoint our Alpha.

Thanks to the blatantly broken lock on the utility door, we

discerned the boys from the Idaho pack had climbed onto the roof — a safe distance from any disapproving eyes.

We carefully made our way over to them, and they cheered, evidently having already taken some of the drugs.

"Sh!" Noah hushed, laughing lowly. "You delinquents are going to get us in trouble."

"I thought you weren't joining," Cody taunted.

"We're not joining you in killing brain cells, but we'll keep you company," Noah replied. I was surprised to see him act so responsibly; only some years ago, he probably would have gladly partaken in such an act of rebellion.

"Speak for yourself," I told him, reaching out a hand with feigned confidence.

Angel grinned, pinching his two fingers inside the small bag in his hand and dropping the smallest shavings of the plant onto my palm.

For a moment, I paused, another memory of a dark room filled with languid bodies flashing through my mind once more. "This isn't *pure* wolfsbane, is it?" I asked, peering closer.

"The guy told me it's a microdose of wolfsbane, blended with some other fun things," Cody revealed, "Curbs the negative and amplifies the positive. Less addictive, too."

I nodded to myself, resigned to the idea that a brief oblivion would be a nice reprieve from the memories of Frankie dancing with the other wolves. "How do I...?"

Cody sniffed loudly, giving me the answer I needed.

"Connall..." Noah spoke quietly. "You don't have to—"

I ignored his warning and promptly inhaled the crushed leaves into my nostrils. Immediately, it felt like my skull burst open, and my skin was set aflame. The pain lasted only a second, and in the aftermath, all I felt was a numb tingling all over, a distant twinkling sound in my ears.

Ringing, maybe, from the blast that had just gone through my head. I snorted at the thought.

"Connall," Noah said again, a little louder, "Are you... smiling?"

"Who knew marble could crack so easily?" Cody joked.

I threw my head back with a laugh. I had never felt so free. *Finally,* for maybe the first time in my existence, I felt what it was like to have a soul unburdened. I was completely un-bogged, weightless without a worry about my ex-communication or Frankie...

I laid back and closed my eyes, thinking only of her. Her green eyes, her dark curls, the freckle above her top lip. I'd never been one for art, but in that moment, I truly felt like I could paint her. The work would never do her beauty justice, but it would be something I could be free to admire with abandon.

"He's a goner," I heard Angel say with a giddy laugh, "Are you sure you don't want some, Noah?"

"Someone has to get you idiots off this roof safely," Noah insisted.

They continued to talk, but I could barely hear them. I was lost in my own daydream, chasing after Frankie in a forest. She ran ahead of me, looking over her shoulder with a laugh.

I could practically hear that delicious rasp now.

Noah suddenly shushed the group and my eyes flew open, realizing I *was* hearing Frankie's laughter. I sat up quickly, searching the darkness below.

Frankie was being pulled outside by the two wolves who had fought over her. Though I couldn't see their faces, their accents suggested that they were from one of the southern state packs.

"I really don't need any air," she insisted, removing her arm from their grip.

"Come on, sugar, you've been dancing all night," one of them sneered.

Noah straightened in alarm, his expression darkening. His eyes darted between all of us, indicating he knew the wolf who was speaking, and for reasons unbeknownst to me, he didn't like him.

"Don't call me sugar," she replied, sounding a little more like herself.

"Why, aren't you as sweet?" the other cooed. They were swarming around her like hornets, ready to sting at any moment.

"I promise you I'm not," her voice dropped.

"I'll be the judge of that," the first one declared, daring to move closer, "How about a taste?"

Before I realized what I was doing, I had launched myself off the roof.

"Connall!" Noah yelled after me as Frankie's scream filled the air.

I had meant to land on my feet, but instead, my knees buckled on impact, and I immediately collapsed into a roll to the ground.

"Oh shit!" one of the guys yelled.

"Are you okay?" Frankie demanded, falling to her knees before me. She looked up to search the roof as we heard the frantic footsteps of the boys overhead. They were retreating, their cover blown.

I sat up on my hands, blinking repeatedly to focus my eyes.

"Where'd they go?" I grumbled, looking around for the two wolves that were no where in sight. I could still take them. I just needed a moment to get the world still again.

"They ran off, you weirdo! You just dropped from the sky like a dead body." Her hands moved to the sides of my face as she searched my eyes.

"Did they hurt you?" I demanded. *I would avenge my goddess to the death.*

"How can you possibly be asking about me when you just *fell off a roof?!*" she retorted, "And what's up with your eyes? Your pupils are huge."

"The better to see you with, my dear," I replied with a sardonic smile.

She sat back on her heels, looking at me in wonder. "You're high," she murmured.

"I am not!" Before I could defend myself further, I turned, and quite unfortunately, projectile vomited. My entire dinner sprayed against the ground with a guttural roar.

Well, if I had *been high, I certainly wasn't anymore.* How quickly the euphoric sensation had passed... I gripped the sides of my head with a pained moan as regret and shame overwhelmed me.

Angel may have misjudged the correct portions of a *micro-dose.*

"I never thought wolfsbane was ever worth trying," Frankie continued with little sympathy, "But now, seeing this, I've been thoroughly scared straight. Thank you."

"French." I wiped my mouth as I begged for help, for mercy.

"Come on," she said with a sigh, reaching for my arm. She helped me up and the moment we were vertical, my eyes connected with a new figure approaching.

Ceallach.

"Perfect," I muttered under my breath.

"Well, well, Connall," my long-lost brother admonished as he approached, "Father will be pleased to hear this is what's become of you: Another O'Faolain junkie for devil's helmet, throwing up outside the party. How *typical.*"

"Oh, fuck off," Frankie spat before I could say anything, "Why don't you do what you're best at and leave him alone?" The entire Summit my family had steered clear of me.

"The *mouth* on you!" Ceallach replied in pretend admonishment, "Connall, is this your mate?"

I wanted to say *yes.* I wanted to lie just to shut him up. I wanted him to see the beautiful, ferocious soul I had been paired with, to know I had the envy of all the wolves here because *she* was *mine.*

Instead, I hung my head in shame.

"Oh, no," he realized with a laugh. "Still a mateless sap, are we?" He stepped forward suddenly, gripping Frankie's chin in his hand and forcing her to look him directly in the eyes.

I growled. My teeth may have barred but my eyes were wide in fear of the worst possible outcome I could ever imagine: *If Frankie Arrowed on my brother...*

"Pity," Ceallach said to my immense relief, dropping his hand.

"Touch me again, and I bite off a finger," she replied, her tone full of venom. Were it not for the fact she was helping me stand upright, I was sure she would've reached for his throat with claws.

"So vicious... you could never be Connall's mate. It is nice to know he has a *little protector.* Christ knows the dope needs it." He kept walking, not saying anything else.

There would be no pleasantries between us, no catching up. My own brother, acting like I was just an acquaintance, someone to sneer at in passing.

"No offense," Frankie murmured as she helped me walk in the other direction, "But I hate your family."

"*You* are my family, French."

She stopped walking and looked at me, some unknown emotion in her eyes.

Maybe I was still drugged. Looking at her, I felt drawn to her lips, and despite having just vomited, I thought to try and kiss her.

Noah and Milo broke through the doors, tearing my attention away.

"Noah told me what happened. Are you okay?" Milo asked, immediately taking my other arm over his shoulder.

"That was quite the fall," Noah added, taking Frankie's place on the other side. I was grateful for the assistance but immediately missed the feeling of her body up against mine.

"He threw up. I think he might have a concussion," Frankie added, crossing her arms. "We should keep him awake until he heals."

"I'm *fine*," I insisted, "It's just the wolfsbane. I don't think it's for me."

"I could have told you that," Milo said with a sympathetic smile, "I made that mistake last time, remember guys?" He looked at Frankie. "Go back to the party. We can take care of him."

"Were you having any luck?" she asked, already knowing the answer. If Milo had Arrowed, he wouldn't be out here with us.

"I'm gonna keep trying," he promised.

"I think I've tried enough," she revealed, to my utmost relief. "Maybe we should just go to the ice cream bar instead."

The others agreed, and halfway there, I found I had regained my proper footing. By the time we reached the doors, the spinning had stopped almost entirely, though I still felt a little *giddy*.

"Hey," I murmured, holding Frankie back as the others moved inside the late-night buffet. "Would you dance with me?"

"What?" she asked, looking around, "Now?"

"Whenever," I expanded, raising a heavy shoulder.

"Whenever." She affirmed with a soft laugh. "But first, let's get you hydrated." She rolled her eyes with a smile, pulling me inside.

"I'm going to hold you to that," I vowed as I stumbled after her.

PART FOUR

The Fifth Year

CHAPTER 11

Frankie

Wolfsblood was busy. Two separate business conferences meant two separate groups of aimless idiots that I had to deal with at the front desk. These kinds of shifts brought out the very worst in me.

It didn't help that I was working with the most distractingly handsome statue ever created, and half the guests were flirting with him right in front of me.

And why shouldn't they? Another year of our love purgatory had passed, and I *still* had to bitterly remind myself I had no claim to Connall. Especially since he pulled away from me. We had once joked about running away together, but the moment we returned from our trip to Mexico, Connall became strangely distant. For the better part of the year I'd fought against his retreat and tried to cling to him. I knew he truly wanted his space when he stopped visiting me in the barn.

Now, the most time we spent together was at nightmarish shifts such as the one we found ourselves in.

"Your name is *Connall?*" I overheard a flirtatious guest asked. She pushed up against the tall counter, placing her hands under her chest to prop up the goods for him.

I was relieved to see his eyes didn't glance down once.

"Yes, ma'am," he replied in his usual straight and dutiful tone.

"I get the sense you're from Ireland?" she asked as if she were some Seer witch openly revealing her power.

"I am," he replied.

I snorted, covering the sound by clearing my throat and focusing on the male guest who had stepped up, asking for another map. He'd apparently lost his original copy in the woods... the third occurrence of the day. One of the groups had decided to do an impromptu hike, meaning we would likely be doing some search & rescue before sundown.

I wrapped up with my guest, making sure to add extra circles to the areas where he was permitted to roam. I was privately pleased to see Connall was equally prompt in finishing up the conversation with his. She had continued to try flirting, but he gave her nothing in return.

I supposed, in a way, I was no better than her. He clearly wanted nothing to do with me, and yet I'd spent most of the morning staring at how his biceps stretched the sleeves of our uniform polo shirt. My fingers itched to reach out and touch him just to see if my hand still perfectly met the curve of his muscle.

Wincing away the thought, I covered my face with my hands and groaned.

"Everything okay?" Connall murmured to me the moment we were left alone.

"I don't know why they continue to put me at Guest Services," I snapped, slapping extra maps onto the counter before anyone else could ask for one. "I *hate* these shifts."

He blinked once in response, unable to offer any agreement.

"*Please*, Connall," I pleaded, "Complain about *something*. Commiserate with me!"

He opened his mouth, but not even a breath came out. I groaned once more. He'd lived on the ranch for *five years* now and still acted like the World's Most Grateful Guest. I so often felt chastened by his integrity.

"Wouldn't you rather we be at the lake?" I tried once more to tempt him to the dark side, stepping closer to him with a smile. "Away from the riff-raff, only having to watch over a family or two. listening to the peaceful lapping of the lake against the rocky shore. Doesn't that sound nice? Isn't this shift the *worst* in comparison to that?"

"I..." was all he could say, his blank stare a little more dazed than usual.

I looked away with a sigh, my eyes catching his admirer returning to the desk. This time, she brought *friends*, like Connall was some zoo animal for them to ogle. I smiled vindictively, welcoming the outlet for my frustration.

"Connall," the woman beckoned him forward, "I was *just* telling my friends how *wonderful* and *helpful* you'd been."

"It's our pleasure, ma'am," he replied, delayed in returning his attention to her.

"See, girls? He's so sweet and *accommodating.*" She licked her lips. "I was telling them all about you, how you're a true Irishman..."

I rolled my eyes.

"I've lived here for a while, ma'am," he answered politely.

"Do you still wear a kilt from time to time?" she purred, "Maybe... *hang loose?*"

As the ignorant women cackled like a pack of hyenas, I stepped forward, the words tumbling out before I could stop them. "Connall usually keeps it in his pants. I suggest you ladies do the same."

I felt him tense beside me, an odd sensation to gather from a man already made of marble, but I walked away as if it hadn't happened. Moving swiftly, I made my way from behind the counter and headed right out the doors to the back porch.

An anger rose in my chest, and I knew what was coming. I just had to get somewhere safe before it happened. My ears were ringing so loud with the precipice of a rage-shift that I almost missed the sound of Connall coming up behind me.

Of all the times for him to suddenly want my company again.

"Don't follow me," I threatened through my teeth as I made my way down the steps to the clearing.

"What is going on with you today?" he asked, moving quickly to stand in front of me and block my path.

"I'm sorry," I spat, my tone indicating I was anything but, "Did I interrupt something? Did you *like* those guests harassing you?"

"Of course not," he said immediately, "But you can't just go verbally assaulting them."

"Why not?" I demanded. "You've intervened before when guests were inappropriate to me!"

"That's different."

I crossed my arms, my brows dropping as I worked to keep my breath steady. The rage was taking over. I couldn't think clearly or see anything other than red. Words spilled out of me before I even knew what I was saying, "Well, aren't you a true knight in shining armor? How about you save your chivalry for someone else because I sure as hell don't need it!"

Before he could react, I bumped his shoulder with mine as I stormed off into the woods. Once I was a safe distance away, I let the rage run through me, and on a shiver, I painfully shifted through my clothes and broke into a run.

After a couple of miles circling the safe areas of the woods, I was able to think clearly again. When the reality of what I'd done sank in, a deep shame overwhelmed me. I couldn't believe at my age I was still rage-shifting like a brand new wolf.

I wasn't sure if it felt the same way for the others. There were times I couldn't *help* but lash out. It was like one minute I was minorly annoyed or frustrated, and the next, there was something powerful inside of me trying to bust its way out with a batting ram.

Whatever that force was, it never broke through, and even after a rage shift, I didn't feel its pressure against my chest any less.

Deep down, I suspected I knew what it was that plagued me. Wolf shifters were meant to find their mate, and every year that I didn't, every year that I wanted *someone else more,* someone who barely gave me the time of day anymore, the wolf in me became more agitated.

I shifted back and crouched over the wooden box mounted in the tree. It was stocked with clothing for shifting emergencies such as this. As I moved, I remained hyper-conscious of my surroundings. Maggie was sure to give me a lecture about my treatment of guests. If one of them caught me streaking in the woods, it would be a full verbal flogging.

Once I was certain the coast was clear, I stood and opened the box, peering inside.

"Shit."

CHAPTER 12

Connall

I knew I shouldn't go after her when I'd been so careful to keep my distance, but it had been too long for her to be out on a run. It was cold, and it was going to rain. Perhaps she was testing me, seeing if I would seek her out like the *true knight* I was.

If she only knew the thoughts that I had of her... I was no knight. I was the villain. Especially after the Summit, I felt unsuitably justified that she hadn't Arrowed, even moreso incited to claim her heart as mine, our pack laws and her future soulmate damned to hell for all I cared. The possessiveness and passion that coursed through my veins for her became so overpowering that I had to stop seeing her alone, for fear I would sink myself inside her and never let her go.

I knew I would cross any line to make her mine, but I couldn't ask her to do the same.

She didn't want to run away with me, she made that much clear with her joke about the circus. Even so, the intense desires that coursed through me the more I tried to stay away... the things I did to her in my dreams... she was wrong to think me noble.

I stopped by the lockers to change out of my work clothes before I made my way into the woods. It was entirely likely she had gone home after her run, but something told me she was still in the trees, as though even outside my wolf form, I could still track her whereabouts.

Sure enough, after only a few short moments, I found her. At the sound of my weight cracking branches beneath me, she flew up in surprise from where she'd been crouched behind a bush.

She had leaves and brush tangled in her curls, and when I saw how her arms protectively held herself from my view, I realized she was also topless.

My throat tightened as I immediately looked anywhere else. "Just what are you up to now, French?" I asked through my teeth.

"Don't give me that tone," she rasped, "It's not my fault! There's no shirt in the clothing box, and I can't cross the path to the other one because a hundred lost city slickers are scattered across these woods like rats."

I looked up at the opened wooden lockbox in the tree and confirmed her story. Someone had forgotten *some* of the wolves on this land needed *more than just pants* after shifting. I refrained from sharing my theory that it was Benji, but failed to hold back my smile. "So, your plan was just to sit behind the bush until nightfall?"

"Are you going to give me your shirt or not?"

Immediately, I pulled my t-shirt over my head. As I began to stretch out my hand to her, I paused, suddenly hoping I hadn't sweat too much in the pre-rain humidity.

A sudden motion from her caught my attention, and I looked up to see that she had dropped her hands and reached an arm out for the shirt. "You think this is funny?" she asked. "You want me to grab it myself? Suit yourself." Her tone was confident as she stood upright, but the red that flushed across her bare chest said otherwise.

Her bare chest.

I turned as quickly as I could, facing away from her completely. I clenched and rubbed my eyes as if it could somehow erase the life-shattering vision I had just seen. For so many years, all the times she had shifted by me, I'd been successful in avoiding this very dreaded thing.

"Jeez, Con, you really know how to make a girl feel special," she muttered, finally covering herself up.

I could say nothing, too busy focusing my mind to think about anything else, something to replace the memory... but it was too late. It was imprinted on my mind: a beautiful, angry, half-naked goddess standing before me like Eve in the garden, tempting me with all that was forbidden. It would forevermore haunt my sweetest, most damned dreams.

Our kind were not meant to take notice of such things; our naked human forms were as natural as our wolf bodies. With Frankie, it was just another rule I would happily break and hate myself for it.

"You're lucky it was me who found you," I said aloud to break the tension. I couldn't dare to imagine how I'd react if I'd taken in the vision from some other wolf's mind.

"Am I?" she questioned, stepping out from behind the bush. The shorts on her bottom were equally as large as my shirt on her, and she had to hold the waistband up in a clenched fist.

"Could've been Milo on a shirtless run," I explained, trying to keep my thoughts from picturing the two of them, "At least I was wearing a shirt."

"God forbid your alabaster skin catch any part of the sun," she murmured, her eyes flicking to the side to take in my bare chest.

I fisted my hands to restrict the urge to cover myself, uncertain if her comment was an insult.

"What were you doing over here anyway?" she asked as we began to make our way back.

I was silent.

"...Looking for me," she guessed with a steady tone.

I held my breath and waited for another biting remark to cut me.

She stopped walking as if sensing my frailty. "Connall," she said, her tone void of any anger. Her temper was finally dissipating.

I looked at her, keeping my face still.

"Thank you."

Before I could react, she laid a hand on my chest, leaned over, and laid a small kiss on the side of my face.

The warmth of her kiss spread across my cheek, and I found myself unable to breathe or move as I watched her begin to walk away from me.

Robotically, my legs pulled me after her.

"Ropes," I said as my stride met up with hers.

"Sorry?"

"That's the shift I cannot stand," I clarified. "Milo asked me to fill in for Noah as his partner one time, and I was terrible at it. I hated having to touch people and jerk them about to make sure their harnesses were on tight. Not to mention the *encouragement* Milo expected me to give them. 'Go on. Keep your balance. You can do it.'" My words came out empty and emotionless, and she burst into laughter at the impression.

"That's truly how I said it," I insisted, "I couldn't bring myself to be any more convincing."

"You're such a downer." Her sarcasm was thick as she shoved my arm playfully. "Just do the job and quit complaining all the time, why don't you?"

I almost smiled, rubbing the back of my neck.

"Hang on," she said with a sudden thought, "Our shift isn't over. Who's at the front desk if we're both here?"

"I snagged a townie," I revealed, using our private nickname for the ranch's human employees. "Kate said she didn't mind giving me a hand."

"Because she's obsessed with you," Frankie scoffed, "She probably thought you intended to work *alongside* her."

"Agh, really?" I grimaced, feeling guilty.

"You truly don't notice how these women throw themselves at you?"

I sighed. "It's of little consequence to me."

"Wish I could say the same," she muttered so quietly I almost didn't catch it. "Well, I'm in no state to return, and neither are you." She gestured to my bare chest. "So, whaddya say we—"

"French," I admonished, following her train of thought.

"Come on," she pleaded, stopping our walk to place her hand on me. I could fight my own desires, but I would do anything she asked when she touched me and looked at me that way. "By the time we get home and change again, the shift will be *so* close to over it would be pointless to go back. The desk is covered. We're *free*. Let's go swimming."

"It's going to rain." I gestured to the ominous clouds above us.

"And lake water is *wet*," she countered. "So what does it matter? No one has to know. Just between us?" She bit back her smile as she took my hand and pulled me deeper into the woods, toward the private lake entrance.

"You're the devil on my shoulder," I said, allowing myself to be seduced without question, "An evil temptress forcing me to complain and abandon my work."

Amongst other temptations.

She grinned wickedly. "I see it differently, Con," she countered, "I think I'm your guardian angel, blessing you with *fun.*"

As if the sky had split open with a loud crack, a sudden and heavy stream of rain poured down upon us.

"This is fun to you?" I yelled to my dark-haired angel over the downpour.

She threw her head back with a laugh, allowing the rain to cascade onto her face without care. When her chin came down, and her eyes met mine, I felt overcome with a roguish urge to push her up against the tree beside us. To catch her gasp on my tongue as I claimed her mouth with mine. To rip away my shirt that now clung to her wet body and replace its contact with my skin instead. To grip her hips, dig my thumbs into the softness of her skin until my fingers left a bruised imprint that marked her as *mine*.

Her mouth opened slightly, and her chest rose and fell quickly with increased breaths. I swallowed harshly, my eyes falling hungrily on the movement, remembering the sight that was now hidden my shirt and wanting to reach out a hand and embrace her in my palm. When I dragged my gaze away and met her gaze once more, she looked as though she could read every one of my thoughts, as if they were etched into my eyes.

"Hello?!" a stranger yelled, interrupting us.

We turned away from each other to see a lost guest, haplessly attempting to use his map coverage from the onslaught of the storm.

"Well, fuck," Frankie cursed.

"Come on, French," I said with a sigh as we waved and jogged over to help him. Perhaps *this* man was my true guardian angel, protecting me from sin.

PART FIVE

The Sixth Year

CHAPTER 13

Connall

I wrapped myself in my comforter as I moved around my small home. A major snowstorm had set in, and despite everyone's invitations to shelter at their's, I'd insisted I would be okay in the cabin.

I hadn't considered that the power might go out or that the rickety structure might not retain much heat. The small heater I had running was low on propane, and it was too intense a storm to attempt to chop any more wood for the fireplace. I just had to bundle up and hope the worst of it would pass soon.

There was a harsh pounding on the door, and at first I assumed it was the wind... until I heard a familiar raspy voice calling my name.

Incredulous that I could have a visitor, I opened it to discover Frankie on my porch, wrapped in a long, puffy jacket... and nothing else. I blinked repeatedly, wondering if I was dreaming. After so many surprise visits from her on my doorstep, it was a script my most secret fantasies expanded on often.

"Change of plans," she announced by way of greeting. She pushed past me and entered the cabin, quickly shutting the door behind her. Her bare feet danced against the cold. "I had initially come to rescue you, but I think we're staying until it calms down a bit."

"Where are your clothes?" I blurted the thought as it echoed a thousand times in my mind.

"It was easier to make it over as a wolf, and I could only fit the jacket in my mouth," she explained lightly.

Before my brain could catch up to the implications of what lay beneath that single layer, I raced to fit her with as many clothes as I could find—sweatpants, socks, a thermal shirt, and a knit sweater. Once she had all she needed, she moved to the bathroom to change. I looked around the cabin in her absence, feeling a frantic panic.

Us, alone in my cabin, snowed in together... It was a better scenario than I'd ever allowed myself to dream up, and for that very reason, we couldn't stay here.

"I told you we should've stayed at my house," she called out from behind the door, as if hearing my thoughts out loud. Despite how much distance I had put between us, she held onto her uncanny knack for reading my mind.

"*You* should've stayed there," I amended, "Why have you come?"

"*I told you,*" she repeated, re-entering the room, "I came to rescue you."

She was gathering her hair into a messy updo, and some untameable curls fell loosely around her face. I sighed in admiration, unnerved by how much the green wool in the sweater brought out the green in her eyes.

My darling one.

Hearing the thought, I winced. *No. Not 'my' anything.*

"Everyone's having a fun little sleepover," she continued, crossing the room to inspect the propane levels of the small heater, "and waiting out the storm together. I didn't want you to be left out."

"I appreciate that, French, but as you can see, I'm perfectly fine. You needn't have risked the frostbite."

"You have no power," she insisted, "And you're running low on gas. You are *not* fine. I don't know why you insist on staying in this shack of a cabin, anyway. We don't even host guests in this area anymore for this exact reason."

"Did you bring some extra propane in your teeth?"

"Unfortunately, not."

"Then I'm no better with you here than I am without."

She glared, the viper ready to strike. "Fuck you. I'm trying to help."

I stood my ground. "It doesn't *help* me in any way for you to put yourself in harm's way—"

"It's only *snow*, Con," she interrupted, "and if you recall, I can harness a *fur coat* at will. Once it dies down a little, we can head back to my house. It's not a big deal."

I was silent, blinking as I fought for an idea of what we were meant to do in the meantime, something that could possibly be sufficient to distract me from the *most pervervid desire* of what I wanted to do with Frankie alone in my cabin.

"Want to make a fort?" she asked, her eyebrow lifting with excitement.

I almost snorted in disbelief at the stark contrast between our mindsets. Sometimes, she seemed so full of light. It was hard not to feel blinded by it. I opened my mouth, unable to come up with an answer.

She read my silence. "I can show you. Benji and I used to make them all the time. It's the perfect snow day activity."

Sometime later, we found ourselves standing before a small fort comprised of blankets, pillows, and the little furniture I had. The heater lay on the floor in the center, and with the surrounding fabric, we would be sufficiently warmed.

"So… what do we do now?" I asked warily, "Apart from sit in it?"

She laughed at the question. "Well, what do you have to read?" she countered, moving to survey the bookshelf.

"Not much, I'm afraid."

"Really? But you're such an avid reader."

"I don't own many," I revealed. "I borrow them." I had almost read through the ranch's library twice. It was a small collection reserved for guests, and I was not in a position to keep any favorites.

"You have a *rock* collection instead of books?" she asked, staring at the stones on my shelf.

"It's not a rock collection." I moved to stand beside her. I gathered the small stones in my arms, gesturing for her to sit in the fort.

She eyed me cautiously but obliged me anyway.

Once she was settled in the warmth of the covered area, I joined her. Gently, I reached for her hand and moved it so that her palm lay flat.

"I used to do this all the time when I was a kid," I murmured, kneeling before her. I placed the largest rock at the center of her palm. Then I added another, gliding it over the grooves until it found stationary balance. "I loved to gather all the rocks around the cliffside and bring them together. Their grooves were always so different, and yet their nature always found a way to connect them to one another." I added the third rock, the stack growing. I shrugged. "It's calming for me, working with gravity, feeling the hard surfaces catch on one another and form these bonds. Seeing the different shapes the stacks make, what it looks like from different angles."

She held her palm firm, her wide eyes watching me as I worked to build the small pile.

"Look." I was almost whispering once I was done. I used the tip of my finger to gently push on the top. The rocks did not move, still connected. "They're stronger together."

She was silent, and I raised my glance to meet her eyes, finding myself suddenly frozen by the emotion in her gaze.

"Con," she whispered.

"French." I swallowed harshly.

"You're just so unbelievable sometimes." She dropped her hand, the rocks clattering to the ground.

I felt my neck warm, embarrassed to have spoken so openly about something so unbearably lame. My brothers had taught me well enough growing up that stacking rocks was not something that was interesting to *anyone* else.

Suddenly, her arms were around me, and she was pulling me to her, enveloping me in a hug.

My eyes widened in surprise, my hands moving to gently hold her arms to me.

"How can you say such things and not see it?" she murmured, pulling away.

"See what?"

"You and I, and everyone in the pack," she explained, "We're just like those rocks. Forged separately but stronger together. You could be a part of us, but instead, you choose to alienate yourself."

I sat back, curling my legs inward, embarrassed to be truly seen by her. Despite all my walls, the depths in which I buried my feelings... somehow she could see parts of me I couldn't even see myself.

"That's all I've ever known, French," I revealed. "My family—"

"At the Summit, you said I was your family. Did you mean that?"

I could only stare, unable to come up with words.

She sighed. "I guess you were high at the time. Are we *friends?*"

I blew out a breath. After so many years, I didn't know what we were. *Friends? Star-crossed lovers? Enemies?* It depended on the day.

"I think we're more than just friends," I answered guardedly.

She was silent, and my heart hammered in my ears until she relented and gave me the smallest nod. "Yeah," she affirmed softly, taking my hand and upturning my palm. She worked on placing the first rocks down before placing one on top of it, and my heart warmed as I watched her work to find the balance. "Ever since the Summit, when none of us Arrowed, I've felt so *angry*. I've basically been pissed off at the world for two years. And you..."

I swallowed harshly, nodding. I'd not just withdrawn from Frankie, I'd pulled away from everyone.

She continued, her delicate fingers picking up the next rock, "But I've come to realize, whatever this connection is between us, whatever it means, it is *good*. It may even be the greatest thing. I feel stronger when you're with me. Even when you used to just silently loiter around the barn while I worked, my days were better with you there. I just wish you could lean on me, or our friends, to be that same strength for you. We can show you how a pack is meant to be if you just learn to trust these connections to support you."

She dropped the final rock on top, eyeing her work proudly.

"That's quite the metaphor," I commented, unable to look away from the smile on her face.

"Then I suppose I don't need to add in everyone's comments about you being made of stone."

A loud static interrupted us, and Benji's voice echoed in the cabin:

"Star Captain, do you read me? Over."

"I'm sorry... what was that?" I asked, restraining a surprised laugh.

"Oh, right, I forgot!" She jolted, searching the fort for where we'd laid out her parka. Reaching deep in the pocket, she fished out a small walkie-talkie. "Moon Cadet, this is Star Captain. I read you loud and clear. Over."

"What are these codenames?" I pressed.

She moved back to her place by the heater, ignoring me.

"Thank God," Benji's voice came through the static, *"Mom was getting worried. Did you make it to Connall?"*

"Yes, but the storm's a little crazy at the moment, so we're going to sit tight until we can make it back."

"Okay, well, you're missing out on hot cocoa."

"And you're missing out on an amazing fort."

"What?! That's not fair!"

"Star Captain signing off, over and out," she replied before shutting off the device.

"They knew you were coming here?' I asked incredulously. *A private visit to my quarters had been sanctioned?*

"I told you it was a rescue mission," she reiterated, "We all care about you. So maybe try working with gravity instead of fighting against it."

I sighed. "You can let go of the metaphor, Frankie. I get it."

CHAPTER 14

Frankie

We were quiet for a bit and just listened to the whistling of the storm outside. The wind was getting lighter, but I wasn't eager to leave just yet. I felt like these moments of silence with Connall were the only times I truly felt at peace. It was a shame I had to ruin it by blurting out the next thought that occurred to me:

"Connall, you really need to get our interior designer up in here. It's been long enough."

"What do you mean?"

"How can you stare at these bare walls all day?"

"It's not so bad."

"Be honest. Don't you want any art to look at?"

"I *have* art to look at," he insisted defiantly. He quickly exited the fort, and I heard the sound of a drawer opening behind me. Returning to his seated position, he passed me a sheet of paper in triumph.

It was the sketch I had drawn on the first day of the science class we'd shared. On the day of our final exam, I'd given it to him as a joke, never imagining he'd keep it.

Not only that, the paper was smooth and soft to the touch over where I'd signed my name and the date. I couldn't imagine how frequently his fingers had to rub against the edges to achieve such a texture.

"How often did you look at this?" I asked, my voice barely a whisper.

His neck reddened. "A couple of times. It was all I had to look at, so maybe you're right— I should get some art." He refused to look at me as he nodded anxiously.

He was embarrassed, and it was only fair that I come clean myself.

"Just between us..." I said softly.

He lifted his head, curiosity in his gaze. "Just between us...?"

"It's you," I revealed.

He blinked twice. "Sorry?"

"The wolf." I turned the paper to face him. "It was you I was drawing. Any time I sketch a wolf, it always ends up looking like you."

Our eyes connected over the paper, and for a moment, I thought the cabin's power had returned from the surge of electricity that went through me. As wrong as it was, I was thrilled we still had moments like this. Where we looked at each other without pretense and wordlessly acknowledged the fire was still there between us. After so many years, it was still there.

Just between us.

"We should go," he said gruffly after a long, thick pause.

"Yep," I agreed, my tone a little too high.

Without any more words exchanged between us, we made our way out into the snow and shifted, both of us carefully controlling our thoughts. Once more, I could only bring my parka in my teeth on the journey back to the house, so I was very relieved to discover some clothes had been set out for us on the front porch. Next to our two piles of layers, a sloppily written sign:

Meet us out back.

"Great, here we go," I warned aloud after I shifted quickly. I turned my back from him and dressed in the pile of layers quickly. A little too quickly, evidently, as when I turned back around, I was met with the image of Connall's broad and bare chest. Unwittingly, my eyes followed it down his abs to the V of his hips and his barely covered—

He caught me staring and yanked the snow pants up higher, turning away from me.

"Sorry!" I winced, turning away as well, "Uh, let me know when you're ready."

"I'm ready," he replied after a moment.

Both of us blushed so furiously that I wondered if we even needed all the layers for our heated skin.

"Come on," I encouraged him to follow me around the house. We had barely turned the corner when an onslaught of snowballs soared through the air, aimed directly at our face.

"You fuckers!" I yelled with a laugh, pushing Connall out of the way. We dove behind a tree as I frantically started gathering snow in my fists.

"Where are they?" Connall murmured, all stoic business as he joined me in the endeavor.

"Behiiiind you," an ominous voice bellowed.

Milo had snuck up behind us, carrying a condensed pile of snow in his arms with Noah on his flank.

Before either of us could react, Milo opened his arms and dropped the snow right on top of us. I collapsed under its weight, the cold and wet ice seeping into my hair and dusting my eyes and cheeks as it broke apart on top of me.

"You'll pay for that!" Connall yelled, gathering up his snowballs faster.

Milo ran away with squealed laughter, seemingly unaffected by the edge of seriousness in Connall's tone.

"Should've watched your back," Noah advised with a shrug, throwing his last snowball over his shoulder as he ran in the other direction.

Connall sent a snowball that hit Noah square in the back.

"Ha!" I taunted him, "Should've watched *yours!*"

"Come on," Connall muttered, taking my hand in his, "We're too vulnerable in this position. Let's take the high ground."

I allowed him to pull me around the perimeter of the yard, my heart beating fast for reasons beyond the thrill of a childish snowball fight. The way he avenged me and the feel of his large hand—

"This is our spot!" Benji yelled, and I ripped my hand away to protect my face from the snowball his friend Finn chucked right at us.

Connall stepped in front of me, taking the brunt of it, prepared with a snowball of his own. "Surrender, Benji," he threatened, raising his hand. "You don't want this fight."

"Yes, I do!" my brother argued.

"Truce!" Noah called, suddenly appearing by the back door, "Aunt Bree just made another round of hot cocoa."

Suddenly, my brother's loyalty to his post was all but forgotten.

Sometime later, I was warmed by a hot mug of hot cocoa in my hands and company around the table. I had succeeded in my mission. Benji and his friend Finn were to my left. Milo and Noah to my right. And Connall was right beside me, nestled between.

If we could stay like this, maybe things wouldn't be so bad. If it always stayed this way, maybe someday, it would feel like enough.

So long as nothing changed.

PART SIX

The Seventh Year

CHAPTER 15

Connall

Noah had Arrowed. After witnessing a wolfsbane attack on his mother, he'd angrily driven to some random park, glanced at a stranger sitting before him, and Arrowed.

As if it were that easy.

"You had to be there," Milo was telling Frankie and me once he found us in the barn. He'd just gotten out of a meeting with the pack elders to discuss the implications of the event. "Noah got all slack-jawed and was panting like he'd been shot up with some kind of stimulant."

"And she's human?" Frankie questioned, crossing her arms. She hadn't looked me in the eye since Milo first arrived, and I was dying to sense her true feelings.

"Definitely human," Milo affirmed. "But that's all we know. He barely said anything to her; he doesn't even know her name."

"How's he going to find her again?" I wondered aloud.

"He says he can feel a *pull* toward her," Milo replied, "I'm sure he'll track her down eventually."

"This is unbelievable," Frankie grumbled, throwing her tool down on her work table with a clatter.

"It's great, though, isn't it?" Milo insisted, "It means the bond is possible for us! It means our soulmates *are* out there... we just haven't met them yet. Hey — maybe they're all human!"

I stared at my feet, suddenly void of any desire to read Frankie's expression. My heart couldn't take it if she agreed with him.

You're not her soulmate. This finally proves it. How often had I rationalized my devotion to her, thinking the Arrows had ended for good? But the magic existed... and it hadn't connected us.

"So, are we going to convene in the woods and have some big meeting about it?" Frankie asked, her tone very guarded.

"Adeline can't shift yet. The vampire doctor said we should wait until the wolfsbane is through her system completely."

"An attempted assassination of our Alpha and an Arrowing. This is shaping up to be one hell of a Thursday," Frankie muttered. She removed the grease towel that was draped over her shoulder, throwing it to the ground with little care as she stalked off toward the backwoods.

I couldn't help myself. I followed her.

"You don't want to hear my thoughts, Connall," she warned, sensing me behind her without having to look.

I pulled her to face me, surprised to see her eyes were wet. "You're crying?"

"Of course I am," she answered with a humorless laugh, "I'm a sore loser."

I was silent, only blinking, *desperate* to know what she meant by that but unable to speak the words to ask.

"It isn't *fair*," she continued, a tear breaking free and falling down her cheek. "Of everyone, why does *he* get a soulmate? He broke the rules worse than any of us." She pulled me into a hug, holding onto me tightly.

Immediately, I collapsed into the embrace, wondering once more how these feelings between us could be so against our nature when Frankie's physical affection was the only one that ever felt natural to me. Every hug or pat on the back from our friends would stiffen my spine on instinct, but one touch from her and I melted.

"I often wondered," I murmured, my hand moving of its own accord to cup the back of her neck under her mess of curls. "If I didn't Arrow when I came here because I coveted *you* too much. I've wanted you more than any hypothetical soulmate."

"You were young," she dismissed, wrongfully assuming I didn't feel the same.

"So was *he* when he broke the rules," I reminded her, "Even still, I thought maybe because I forsook the bond, I lost the right to it forever. But..." I swallowed harshly, forcing myself to speak the words, "This means there's hope for us."

"There's hope for *you*." She sniffed after her amendment. "And maybe there's hope for me. But there is *no* hope for *us.*"

She pulled away slightly, and my eyes unwittingly drifted down to her lips, drunk on the proximity. I watched her throat bob with a heavy swallow as she read the untimely desire in my gaze.

With a choked sob, she placed a hand on my chest, pushing me back, a firm command not to follow her further as she trudged off into the shadows.

It drove me crazy to see her crying and know there was nothing I could do about it. I turned and dragged my feet back to the barn, running into Noah at the entrance.

"I hear congratulations are in order," I greeted him, mustering as much enthusiasm as I could manage. It wasn't a lot.

Noah opened his arms with a smile, pulling me into a tight hug. "Thanks, man! Now that we know they can happen, I'm sure your Arrow will happen soon."

"One can only hope," I weakly agreed as I pulled away. "So... tell me about her."

"Oh, man, she's the most beautiful girl I've ever seen. Where do I even begin? She has red hair—"

"Is she Irish?" I interrupted.

"No idea. Maybe!" he said, a wide grin on his face. He looked around suddenly, his smile unfaltering. "Where's Frankie?"

"Out for a run. Milo beat you to the news, though."

"That's okay," he replied lightly.

He truly did not have a care in the world. Which was surprising, given the emotional state he had been in when he left the ranch.

"How's your mom?" I asked delicately.

He took a deep breath, the light in his eyes only diminishing slightly. "Better. She and I had a long talk just now. I just can't imagine who would do such a thing to her."

"Nor can I," I agreed, "She has no theories?"

"None at the top of mind."

"Then we'll have to dig deeper," I pressed.

"That's what I said! She seemed less concerned about the whole ordeal simply because she opened the trap in her human form."

"That letter was enchanted to release an inordinate amount of wolfsbane. That's no accident. That's a message." I shook my head before a sudden thought occurred to me, "Would it be alright if I made her something to help? Or— I'm sure the vampire doctor gave her plenty of remedies..."

"Couldn't hurt!" Noah threw his arm around my shoulders, and together, we walked back toward his house. There was only a beat of silence between us before he was talking about his soulmate again. "Did I tell you she was a redhead?"

I knocked on Adeline's office door with one hand, delicately balancing a tray in the other. I was nervous about such a private meeting with her. Rarely was I left alone with my adopted Alpha, a trend of my own creation. I aimed to float under her radar, wanting to avoid her examining me too closely and seeing the same worthlessness my father had.

"Come in." Adeline's voice was soft beyond the wood, void of its usual cadence.

When I opened the door, her eyebrows raised in surprise. "Connall. Did you hear the news?"

"Would be hard not to. I think Noah's just about to sing it from the mountaintop."

Her tired face broke into a full grin. "He's excited," she said with a laugh. "We all are. It's a sign of positive things to come."

I held my breath, forcing a stiff nod. *It was a sign of the opposite for me.* I held up the tray to change the subject. "I made you a cup of something that might help with the wolfsbane."

She sat up straighter with warm excitement. "Tea?"

"If you could call it that." I grimaced, placing the tray down in front of her, "I'd knock it back in one go, and I wouldn't advise smelling it beforehand either."

"This is quite the presentation," she murmured, looking down at the tray. In addition to the teacup, I had added a sleeve of crackers and a flower from her garden.

"The crackers will help with the aftertaste," I explained.

The corners of her eyes wrinkled with her smile. "Well, now I'm well and truly nervous."

"It's something I would make back home for... for those who sometimes needed it," I weakly explained. "There's no pressure to drink it, of course. I just thought it might help." I turned to leave her to it, but her next words stopped me in my tracks:

"Will you sit with me for a moment?"

My heart racing, I moved to the chair opposite her desk. She didn't take the remedy yet but instead clasped her hands and looked at me pointedly.

"I always believed it was rather unfair of your father to send you here to Arrow," she began, "For some time now, this ranch has felt like a loveless land, and every year that you did not find your soulmate, I felt personally responsible for your loneliness. I've often wondered if I should have been more firm with your father."

I was silent, only able to blink out of fear for what she might say next.

She took a steadying breath and continued, "Selfishly,

however, from your very first day here, I've been very grateful to have you in our pack. I understand you prefer to keep to yourself but I hope you know that I see you as a member of my own family. Especially now that we know for certain that Arrows are possible for our pack, I would love nothing more than to see you settled down."

That simple sentiment meant so much, and I swallowed with the uncertainty of how to express it.

"I'm ecstatic for the day you find your soulmate," she concluded, "In the meantime, if there's anything I can do to make you happy... perhaps a feeling or inclination I can will away..."

My spine stiffened, the warmth in my chest dissipating. *Was she insinuating...*

Sensing my confused alarm, she spoke plainly, "I can't promise it'll work, but I can try and use an Alpha command to make your friendship with Frankie more... comfortable."

I was overcome by my shame that despite my best efforts, she had taken notice of my attachment. *She was offering to help? Was that even truly possible? Could Adeline use her Alpha commands to prevent me from caring for Frankie to the extent that I did?*

I tried to imagine a world where those feelings were miraculously shut off, like turning off a tap. Immediately, I jolted, rejecting the notion with my entire body. As painful as it was to love her, I would continue to trudge through the fire and ice until I was absolutely certain Frankie could never be mine.

There was only one right way out of this: One of us would have to Arrow. Until then, I would hold tight to frayed threads of hope.

I blinked repeatedly. "No, ma'am," I said firmly, "I'm comfortable with things as they are."

Adeline sat back in her chair, and while I'd never been an expert in reading faces, I could almost wager she looked oddly pleased with my response.

CHAPTER 16

Frankie

A month passed before I finally started to let go of my jealousy. Noah's soulmate was purely to blame for my change of heart; Sophia Rose was a difficult human not to love. Even after she learned what we were, she approached every wolf on the ranch with warm eyes, a big smile, and literal open arms.

She even pulled *me* into a hug on occasion, and every time it happened, I felt the ice around my heart chip away. It wasn't her fault her presence was a stark reminder that Connall and I were doomed. Or that every time I looked at her and Noah, I felt the desperation for a love like theirs, one that was open and public.

In a twisted way, I was almost grateful for the distraction of a threat against our kind.

Beau had returned to our lives, and the news of his evil-doing around Canada had us all shaken. He was using a witch's magic to *tear* wolves from the magical confines of their pack. It wasn't just ex-communication, it was *exsanguination*, ripping a wolf from their lifeblood against their will.

I couldn't understand it. Beau had left his pack of his own volition, getting beyond the reach of Adeline's Alpha control. Why couldn't he give these wolves that same choice? Even if they survived the ordeal, a Ripped wolf never recovered. Without a pack, the Ripped were without a *soul,* and thus became rabid. It was a senseless cruelty to tear a person from their loved ones and turn them into a maniacal monster.

"This book will make all my wishes come true," Beau had said that night he found me alone in the woods. *Had the threat been right there in front of me? If I hadn't run away, would I be one of the Ripped too?*

"Everything okay?" Connall's voice cut through my worries.

I jolted from my stool in shock. I'd been so lost in the memory I hadn't seen him step inside the barn.

He moved closer, his hands hovering over my arms and I refrained from closing the distance to feel them. After Noah Arrowed, Connall was even more careful with how he touched me.

"What's wrong?"

"Nothing, I'm fine," I insisted, dragging my fingers under my eyes to wipe away the tears I hadn't realized were there. "What's up?"

"Your brother's looking for you." His brows remained furrowed with concern as his eyes searched mine.

"Isn't he always?" I huffed. "What's it about this time?"

"He wants to... I don't know. I think he wants Sophia Rose to ask us all questions."

"What, like, *Interview With A Wolf Shifter?*" I almost felt the threat of a smile. "Is this his way of making up for rage-shifting and scaring the shit out of her?" Shaking my head, I moved to leave the barn, but he held out an arm to halt me.

"French..."

"I'm okay, Con, really," I insisted. "I just have a bad feeling about everything going on in Canada."

He nodded, not saying anything more.

"Connall..." I spoke softly as the anxious thought occurred to me, "It didn't... it didn't *hurt,* did it?"'

"What?"

My eyes flooded again in fear of what he might say. "When you joined us. You've never said... what the process was like."

"No, it didn't hurt, Frankie."

I closed my eyes, releasing a sigh of immense relief.

"But," he continued, "For a brief moment... I did feel lost. Like I was falling into a vast blackness at a speed that sent my stomach to my throat. It felt like my consciousness was getting farther away from my wolf until Adeline called me back. It's not a feeling I would wish on my worst enemy. These Ripped..."

"They're innocent. They deserve to be saved."

He shook his head solemnly. "Frankie, the only thing that can save them is death."

I stared out the window, watching a fierce redhead kick the air and lightly beat her fists against the back of the tall figure that had thrown her over his shoulder.

"Noah's an idiot," I muttered.

Sophia broke free from Noah's grasp for just a moment before he took her back up into his arms and carried her to her car.

"He's terrified like the rest of us," Milo corrected from where he spied beside me. "He just wants to get his soulmate somewhere safe."

Once the couple stopped arguing and started kissing, I dropped the curtain and we turned away.

"Tell us again," Milo prompted the pair of witches standing at the center of the room. Noah's ex-girlfriend Chloe and her coven companion Phoenix had come in abruptly, interrupting Sophia's interview to deliver the worst news imaginable:

"Beau is coming to Wolfsblood with an army of Ripped," Chloe repeated. She looked so *guilty* I wondered if there was more to the story she wasn't sharing.

"How does one even *command* an army of Ripped?" Connall argued, his voice flat. From the moment he heard the news, he had turned to stone, revealing no signs of the trepidation that overwhelmed the rest of us.

"My aunt in Canada has informed me that he found a way to control them," Chloe clarified, "He's set on coming here and..."

"Killing us," I finished for her.

Benji gasped, and I remembered all too late that my little brother was in the room. Quickly, I moved to the couch, squeezing myself between Benji and Connall to give my brother a hug.

"I'm fine," he insisted, shoving me away, but his unfocused stare at the carpet said otherwise.

"And you know this for certain?" Milo affirmed.

Noah re-entered the room just as the witch beside Chloe nodded. Everyone moved to stand, unsure of what to do but just knowing we had to do *something*.

"I have to call a pack meeting," Adeline announced, quickly leaving the room.

Noah gently instructed the witches to leave, and I watched as Chloe lingered, pleading something quietly to Noah with tears in her eyes. She kissed his cheek before she left.

I looked away, my teeth grinding with the truth that there was definitely more to the story that they weren't telling us. I felt myself going down a trail of poisoned thoughts, like *how could Noah be blessed to have a soulmate and still allow his ex to kiss him* when suddenly, a warmth pulled my focus.

Connall had wrapped his hand around mine.

I looked up at him with misty eyes. He remained stony, but the slight flex of his jaw as he looked at me revealed all he felt underneath.

"We're going to be okay, guys," Noah said lamely.

I rolled my eyes. "He's taken control of a pack of *Ripped* wolves, Noah. And our numbers are lower than ever."

"They say the Ripped wolves are the strongest of any," Milo

added, "There's no humanity, no *hesitation* when it comes to killing."

"Don't think like that!" Noah argued, "You're acting like he's already won. This is our territory, and we are going to protect it. So what if he has a witch working for him? You heard Chloe, we have a whole *coven* on our side."

My mouth twisted, thoroughly uninspired by my cousin's rousing speech. Before I could let out another retort, we all were struck with the call of the Alpha.

It was time to come together and plan our defense.

CHAPTER 17

Connall

T tightened the knots I'd made, ensuring the paddle boats were secure inside their mounts on the wall. Wolfsblood Ranch was now closed to guests, but I still wanted to ensure everything was locked up inside the boat house at the lake. It wasn't like knots would matter to a rabid monster with claws and teeth, but I was desperate to do anything to make myself useful.

I also needed a place to hide the emergency getaway bag I packed for Frankie, Benji, and me. It contained just enough supplies that, if it came down to it, I could get Frankie and her brother somewhere safe until the danger subsided.

As I locked up, I looked out at the lake water, wondering what the future held in store for all of us. My thoughts carried me to the edge of the waterline where I sat, my hands mindlessly reaching to gather some stones.

"All set?" a voice called out behind me when I had a sizeable stack built.

I looked over my shoulder to find Milo coming down the hill.

"All set," I affirmed, my hand flashing out to knock the rocks over before he saw it.

He sat down next to me with a sigh. "You enjoy running the lake?"

"I do. Though perhaps not as much as you enjoy running the ropes course."

He looked at me, an edge in his smile. "I didn't always love it," he revealed. "My sister was found dead there."

My lips parted in surprise. I had just hidden something as trivial as a pile of rocks I built, and here he was, baring his soul so openly. I looked out at the soft lapping waves of the lake, feeling miserable that I could not be as open, nor could I articulate any words of condolences for my friend's unthinkable tragedy.

He followed my gaze out at the water. "For a while, I thought maybe if I had been there, I could have somehow prevented whatever happened. I became obsessed with the idea of taking control of that space, running it as safely as possible so that no one would ever be harmed there again. Over time, I learned to let go a little, and the course started looking different. I started to see how it brought groups of people together, the positivity that bloomed after every exercise. How the value it offered outweighed the danger."

"I'm sorry," I finally managed to say.

"It's okay," he assured me, "I guess now that we're facing a sizable risk of death, I find myself thinking about her a lot. I worry about all of us. I worry what this place will feel like after the horrors we're about to witness and how long it will take to feel right again."

I nodded in agreement.

"I don't understand him," Milo muttered after a while. "Beau. Was it not enough cosmic punishment that the Arrows stopped happening for us, and that we're all alone?"

"We aren't alone, Milo." I reminded him. We had a ranch full of shifters that had traveled from all over to help us fight.

Milo's grin widened, and he clapped a hand on my shoulder. "You're absolutely right. Speaking of which, my Colombian cousins are probably getting themselves into trouble. I should probably find them. Is any of your extended family coming?"

I shook my head. Adeline had assured me they were too far

away to rope them into this, and that our numbers were solid and we needn't worry them. Secretly, I suspected she *had* asked, and they declined to help. They were supposed to be our brother pack, and they couldn't offer up any wolves to help us in a desperate time of need. It was shameful.

Milo left shortly thereafter, but I was only alone for a few minutes before another visitor arrived: a young woman from the Alberta pack. Her family had traveled from Canada to avenge her twin brother, who'd become one of the Ripped.

"Oh, hey," she greeted me softly, "I just went for a bit of a mindless walk and found myself here. Do you mind if I join you? I don't really know what I'm meant to do."

"There's not much we can do at this point," I replied.

She sat down beside me, and I straightened my posture uncomfortably. The silence between us didn't feel as congenial as it had with Milo.

"You're Connall, right?" she asked after a moment. I nodded, and she held out a hand. "I'm Zoe."

"It's nice to meet you." I shook it quickly, returning my hand to the rocks beside me. "I'm sorry about your brother."

She nodded stiffly, looking out at the water. "Do you mind if I ask you something, Connall?"

I was silent, uncertain where she was headed.

She kept going, not waiting for my permission. "I heard you switched packs. Was it—"

"It wasn't the same," I interrupted, having received this question too often since we first learned of the Ripped. "I chose this."

She looked away, perhaps taken aback by my firm tone.

I cleared my throat. "What, um, what was he like?"

"Alexandre?" she clarified, "Oh gosh, he's the best of us. I was born a minute before him, but it was immediately clear he would be the next Alpha. He's so tall and calm, both physically and metaphorically, a pillar of strength. I tend to be a bit of a downer, but he is pure sunlight."

I noticed she spoke in the present tense as if the Alexandre she knew was still out there. "Do you know how it happened?"

"No." She looked down. "We used to hike at night a lot. And I do mean *hike*... as humans. We got a thrill from how *spooky* it felt. Sometimes, we'd take diverting paths, but we always found our way back to one another. We never felt there was any real risk of danger. I only wish..." She paused, struggling with emotion. "I wish I had stayed right beside him. Or that we had shifted, because then I could've heard him..."

"Ah-em!" A loud voice called down from the hill.

Zoe and I turned our heads to see Benji standing with his arms crossed. The brazen teenager moved down the hill, stomping his way over to us with over-the-top aggression.

"What's his deal?" Zoe asked quietly.

"I rarely know," I replied honestly.

"Hope I'm not *interrupting*," Benji said, his tone strangely curt, "Just thought you should know, Connall, that *Frankie* is looking for you."

"Is that the scary one with the curly hair?" Zoe asked.

I hid my proud smile as I moved to my feet.

"Yes, *very* scary," Benji affirmed. He moved his hands to my back to push me back toward the hill, glancing at our guest from over his shoulder. "And she's my *sister*, so *watch yourself*."

"Alright, take it easy now," I muttered, maneuvering from his grasp to ruffle his hair. Looking down at Zoe, I said, "Feel free to stay here, where it's peaceful. I find it's a great place to be alone with your thoughts."

"I've had far enough of that," she declined, moving to stand. She looked at our scowling visitor. "If you don't mind, can I tag along? I'm Zoe."

"Benji."

Her smile was friendly despite his cold demeanor. She looked like she almost found it equally amusing and confusing. "Hello, Benji. What's fun to do around here?"

Suddenly, Benji forgot all about what had been bothering him, and he came to life, linking his arm with hers. "Come with me, *mademoiselle*," he said smoothly.

"I know I'm Canadian, but you can skip the French," I heard her say as they strode ahead.

"You're Canadian?" he replied.

I paused, taking one last look at the lake. I was envious that Noah was able to send his loved one to the other side of the country. I knew Frankie would refuse to leave. Packing the getaway bag had been a fool's errand.

CHAPTER 18

Frankie

" I wish shifters could get drunk," I said, staring at the campfire. "It feels like a fitting act to do the night before the end of the world."

"Don't call it that," Milo corrected me immediately.

Ever the optimist, our friend.

"A hangover wouldn't help you in the battle," Benji added.

I smirked at my little brother sitting beside me. "And what do *you* know about hangovers?"

"I watch TV! I know things!"

I shook my head, looking up at Milo, who had stood to stoke the bonfire. "Remind me to set parental controls on our television when this is all over."

"Hey!" Benji protested, "I'm a man now. I can watch whatever I want."

My throat suddenly felt thick as a shiver ran down my back that had nothing to do with the night air. Benji was too eager for what lay ahead, too naive to hold any regard for his innocence. He *insisted* he fight the Ripped alongside the rest of us.

"You're still a kid." I couldn't help myself from trying one last time to stop him. "Which is why I—"

"Give it a rest, will you?!" he groaned, immediately incensed by my words. "I am not staying back to babysit the elders. I deserve to protect our home alongside everyone else!"

"Benji—"

"I wish you'd just shut up about it already!" he yelled, getting up, "You have to stop treating me like a freaking child!"

"Okay! Don't go!" I reached out a hand but failed to stop him from walking away. "I'm sorry, I just—!" My eyes flooded as I watched him disappear down the hill. It was our last night together, and I ruined it.

"I'll get him," Connall said, immediately moving to go after him.

It was down to Milo and me, and he looked after them with a sigh.

I moved my eyes back to the fire. "I know fighting is the last thing we need to do right now. I just... I will not see him become a murderer."

"I know you won't," Milo replied, "You'll protect him."

I would. I would defend Benji until my last breath. I just had to pray *for once in his life* he wouldn't do anything stupid. It could cost me my life.

I continued to stare at the fire, tears still threatening to fall from my eyes.

After some time, Connall and Benji finally came back up the hill, and I jumped to my feet.

"I won't say anymore, I promise." I held up my hands with innocence.

"You're just lucky I have no one else to hang out with at the moment," Benji answered. When he moved back to his seat beside me, however, he bumped his knee against mine to show all was forgiven.

"Do you think Noah and the others will be up all night?" Milo asked. Our parents and the leaders of the other packs were convening with Adeline and Noah in the Main Building to reaffirm the battle plan. "I feel like we should be there, helping."

"Noah's in another tier now," I disagreed. "He's going to be

Alpha, and he gets to participate in the secret plotting sessions. We just have to do what we're told."

I felt an arm around me and turned to see Connall sit on my right, his hand stretching the corner of a flannel blanket to drape over my left shoulder.

I held onto it, relieved at the comfort as he took the other corner to cover his own shoulder.

It was intimate, sharing a blanket like this, and it definitely toed the line. It *crossed* the line that Connall's arm remained wrapped around me, hidden from the other's view underneath the cloak of flannel.

Even if they did see, I knew Milo and Benji wouldn't comment on it.

"Well, *we* should at least get some good sleep tonight if we can," Milo continued. "Let's burn through the logs and call it a night."

When the fire died, Connall insisted on walking Benji and me home.

"Your place is closer," I weakly argued as we walked down the trail side by side. Benji sauntered ahead as if he didn't have a worry in the whole world.

"I don't care," Connall replied. Under the cover of night, he slid his hand in mine, holding it safe with his to prove his point.

I looked away, feeling as though a butterfly made of stone had flipped in my stomach and crashed against my ribs. He'd been so careful not to touch me over the last couple of weeks, and now he was holding me with abandon.

Whatever that meant, it scared the hell out of me.

"Okay, good night then!" Benji called out once we neared the house. He picked up his pace, getting inside our home and closing the door behind him quickly.

I tried not to roll my eyes at his childish dramatics. He was always supportive of Connall and me spending alone time together, but he was a little too obvious in his matchmaking efforts more often than not.

It'd been that way ever since that night I came home and found Benji had been eavesdropping. I was suddenly struck with the image of how *small* he was back then, sitting on the couch in his space print pajamas—

"French." Connall pulled me into a tight hug the moment I burst into tears.

"I know he's not a kid anymore, but he's still so *young*. It isn't fair that he has to face something like this. It isn't fair to *any* of us to go through this!"

"There'll be no stopping him at this point."

"That's what I'm scared of."

He placed his hands on either side of my face, his fingers delving into my hair that reeked of campfire smoke. "Nothing will happen to *either* of you. I swear it."

I moved my hands over his, my eyes silently begging that he kiss me and silence every anxious thought in my mind. *"Connall—"*

"Milo was right. We should get some sleep." He slid his hands away, and without another word, he walked off into the darkness.

Later, as I failed to fall asleep in bed, I kept wondering if that was our last chance, and we blew it. One moment, where we could love each other without any regard for the consequences, and we let it slip away.

CHAPTER 19

Frankie

We burst through his cabin door, and I kicked it shut behind us, locking the deadbolt as if it could do anything to keep the monsters at bay. Connall stumbled toward the bed, one arm wrapped around his side and the other clutching his neck. His palms were futile in stopping the blood pouring from his wounds, and I was frantic to find something to apply more pressure.

I ripped his bed sheet from the bed, tearing it in half with my teeth.

"French," he rasped.

"Shut up, Con, I'm trying to think," I spoke through gritted teeth as I continued ripping the sheet into strips. Once I had enough, I wrapped his neck and then his torso. He winced at the contact as I tightly bound the fabric around him. The sheet flooded with red, and a wave of nausea hit me once I realized the depth of his wounds.

Just adding pressure wouldn't be enough. He was taking too long to heal, and he was losing too much blood.

"How could you do this?" I whispered, tears clouding my vision as I tied a knot in the wrapped fabric and moved him to lie down. "Benji was safe and I had it handled! *Why* did you insist on taking them all on by yourself?"

He reached a bloodied hand to my face, caressing my cheek as the tears spilled over. "F-French," he spluttered.

"Connall, that was a rhetorical question. I fucking mean it, save your energy and stop talking." I ran to the window, looking out through the curtain to ensure no Ripped had followed us. Outside my wolf form, I wasn't sure how many were left or if I would be able to get him to the hospital without any more confrontation.

I looked down, suddenly realizing underneath the smears of dirt and Connall's blood, I was completely naked. I couldn't bother to think twice about that. There was no time for humility. We were safe for now, but we couldn't stay here, or Connall would bleed out.

"Please," he groaned, interrupting my frantic thoughts.

"Connall, *shut the fuck up!*" I yelled, turning back to him. I was near hysterics at the sight of him, losing more of my mind with every second I got closer to losing him.

"Please. C'mere," he said, his tone firm as he held a red hand out to me.

I moved to him, sitting on the edge and holding his bloodied hand in mine.

"I have to say this," he continued, gasping for air, "You have to hear it."

Panic shot through me once more and I shook my head vehemently. "No—"

"I love you, Frances."

My head hung limply.

"I always have, I always will." He struggled to get the words out but persevered through panting breaths, *"Arrow be damned,* you have owned my heart from the moment I first saw you. I know we did not form a bond because you are more perfect than my wretched soul could ever deserve, and yet I have loved you, worshipped you, *craved* you regardless."

There it was... the truth between us that could no longer be buried or forgotten or ignored.

"I love you, Connall," I whispered as I gave into my tears, moving to lay down beside him. "I always did. I never stopped."

"French," he whispered, his eyes fluttering closed.

I moved to kiss him, my tears and his sweat colliding on contact. But his lips could barely move against mine. He was fading from me so quickly.

"You have to live," I begged him, "You can't leave me! Con, I can't go on without you." More tears spilled from my eyes in rejection of the thought. *"You* are my soulmate. My heart and soul are *mine* to give, and I say they're both completely yours. I curse the stars every night for not making you mine in the one way that matters to everyone else. I don't care about whatever bond is or isn't between us. I won't live my life without you!"

His eyes remained closed and I moved my hands to his wounds, praying for the bleeding to slow down.

Give us more time, I pleaded to whatever higher powers were listening. *Please, heal him!*

I felt it then, like a battering ram against my ribs. Some magic inside of me, trying to get out. Following the instinct, I closed my eyes, focusing on his wounds. I willed my own healing powers to leave me and move into him. I didn't need healing powers; he could have them. There would be no healing from a world without him.

He groaned, shifting his position, and I feared the consequences of the movement until I realized less blood was leaking through the wraps.

It was working!

I waited another minute, ensuring the bleeding was truly slowing down, before moving to stand.

"Come on," I said, "We're getting you to a doctor."

He groaned as I helped him get upright again. "You can't— the Ripped—"

"I promise you, no more harm will come to you. If I see a

single beast out there, I will tear out its throat with my teeth." I took a deep breath. "I'm gonna shift to keep an ear to the ground on what's happening with the others. Just lean on me as we go, okay?"

He closed his eyes and nodded, allowing me to pull him to the door.

I opened the door a crack, once again ensuring the coast was clear. "Can you walk?" I asked desperately as I helped him onto the porch.

He nodded once more, more weakly this time as his eyelids fluttered closed.

I sighed. "I don't suppose you'd be open to riding me?"

His eyes flew open with the question.

"I know that's a little unconventional, but I can't help you walk and fight any Ripped at the same time. If you ride my wolf, I can get us there faster."

He swallowed harshly, and I took no more time to decide. I shifted, moving myself below the steps so that he could easily lay upon me.

He stretched himself across my spine, his arms wrapping around me and his fingers clenching to my fur.

Connall's severely injured and not healing fast enough, I reported to whoever could hear me, *I need to get him to help! Where is everybody?*

If you can get to Main, Milo's voice replied, echoing in the distance, *I can get you to the hospital with Noah's truck. We're okay. Some wolves are doing some final patrol, but I think it's over.*

No Ripped left? I questioned.

Most of them died with the full shift, he replied.

My mind flashed to Alexandre, one of the Ripped that attacked Connall. He didn't look anything like we'd expected, half-wolf, half-human, and more zombie than anything else, like he'd become frozen mid-shift. When we had him cornered, he started to shift fully, and the moment he did, he just fell over, dead. It happened to all the Ripped that were provoked into a full shift. It literally killed them to fully transform, as if their very hearts couldn't stand to be a wolf torn from their pack.

"Alexandre?!" a voice screamed. Suddenly, a figure burst through the trees, and I reared my hind legs, growling and gnashing my teeth in warning.

"Holy shit!" the young woman exclaimed once she saw me. She held up her hands as if I were some wild horse that gesture could tame. "It's me, Zoe! Alexandre's sister from Alberta? I'm on your side! Is that, wait— *Connall?!*"

I snarled louder, feeling saliva drip from my fangs. Her brother had nearly killed Connall, and now she was delaying me from saving him.

She stumbled backward in fear from whatever she saw in my eyes, and I sprinted away from her, forcing myself to ignore her helpless calls to her dead brother. There was no time I could waste to extend her any sympathy.

I had to get to Connall to safety before it was too late.

CHAPTER 20

Connall

I knew things had gone horribly wrong when I saw my mother.

She was standing in the sunlight on the edge of a cliff, misty gusts of air blowing her red hair around her like a wildfire. I had never known her likeness outside of photos, but even at first glance, and only seeing her back, I felt in my heart that it was her.

Even so, as I moved to stand beside her, I was too scared to turn my head and face her head-on for fear I could be wrong.

"Am I dead?" I asked, looking down at the magnificent waters that crashed against the mighty rocks below. It had been so long since I'd seen the Irish coastline. Even as the dense clouds moved overhead, enveloping us in the gray, it was more beautiful than I remembered. "Or... is this a dream?"

"Which would you prefer, love?"

I sighed, reveling in the accent that sounded like home and the voice that felt full of a tenderness I had barely come to know. If it *was* a dream, I didn't want to wake up anytime soon. I considered my answer. "If I really died so the one I loved could live... I could be at peace with that."

She turned her head, and I met my mother's eyes for the first time. They were just like mine and the ocean before us, a deep and stormy blue. She gave me a knowing smile. "I couldn't agree more, Connall."

She looked out at the horizon again, but I was not able to turn away.

"Mam," I whispered over the sound of the waves and wind. I choked on the word, my throat thick with the novelty of addressing her. "I'm so sorry. For what I did to you when I was born."

She shook her head lightly, the smile on her face growing sad. "You did nothing, Connall. You were perfect and innocent. It was your..."

But she didn't finish the words, and the clouds parted. Strong sunlight enveloped us, flooding my vision. I winced, raising a hand to cover my eyes as the soft beeping of a machine carried over the wind.

"Connall," Frankie whispered, her voice thick with emotion, "You're in the hospital. I think we lost you for a second, but you're safe now. You're going to be okay."

Even after I came to, my stay in the supernatural hospital remained a blur. I wasn't certain if the vampire doctor kept me heavily medicated through the transfusions, or if it was just my body's way of healing from the severity of my injuries. For whatever reason, I couldn't grasp any passage of time. All I knew was that Frankie stayed by my side throughout it all. She continued to pretend to be mad at me for having protected her in the battle, but the truth was out in the open between us:

We truly loved each other. I would die for her. *I almost did.*

As soon as I was healed, I was determined to propose once more that we run away together, and not to the circus neither. Or maybe Adeline and the pack could accept us, making an exception for our unsanctioned love after witnessing its depth firsthand. Either way, after what we had experienced, I refused to be without her for another day.

I was in the middle of silently weighing both outcomes when Chloe entered with a small plant in her hands. The witch's gift was a nice gesture but of little interest to me. I only half-paid attention to the conversation amongst the group until Milo's voice came in clear:

"What does this mean? It's possible I could have met my soulmate already and not know it?"

Frankie took my hand, and it sent a jolt through me, waking me up from the haze as the words spoken finally seeped into my understanding. *There was a magical block on the Arrows... a curse set upon us by Beau's witch... it was possible...* I allowed myself to look at Frankie, mirrored emotions echoing in her gaze.

"Yes," Chloe answered Milo, "I think I know how to break the curse, too."

Frankie's grip on my hand tightened.

As I dared to hope, I found myself slipping back under.

I dreamt I was back home, inside the small cottage on our property. Voices rumbled behind a closed door, and a familiar putrid smell filled the air: spiced plums, truffles, sawdust, and tobacco. I'd forgotten how bad this building always smelled, and for reasons outside the sheep and pigs. At the manor, we presented ourselves as a distinguished pack, fearsome and powerful. The goatherd cottage was where the real truth could be found. Slowly, I walked along the wall, my ears tuning in to the conversation on the other side of the door.

A loud retching sound entered the air, followed by some yelling and laughing.

Someone was sick?

I raced to enter the room. The moment I peered inside, my presence was immediately rejected by an angry chorus.

"Agh, Connall, *get out!*"

"Christ, he's like a ghost that won't quit hauntin'," my brother Cian groaned.

"Pass it to me again," my brother Cormac gurgled from where he lay on the floor. He rolled over onto his side, spitting the last of his vomit into the straw on the floor. "He ruined my high."

I took in the extent of the mess, discovering my brothers would rather vomit where they lay than do something for themselves. They were more pigs than wolves, rolling around in their own filth.

"Do you want some?" Ceallach asked, holding up the pipe. He sneered at me as if the invitation were a joke. Though he held the pipe, his eyes were strangely clear and sober. *If he wasn't taking any, why should I?*

I shook my head vehemently.

"Leave him be. He couldn't handle it," a deep voice came from the shadowed corner.

I followed the voice, surprised to see my father slumped in his old rocking chair, halfway slipping out of his seat. I'd known my brothers were miscreants, but this was our *father,* our *Alpha,* and he was... partaking in this?

"No," Ceallach agreed with him, passing the pipe over, "He isn't one of us."

I'm certainly not, I wanted to yell. Instead, I shut the door and ran out of the house, their raucous laughter echoing in my ears.

I opened my eyes to the white hospital ceiling. I hadn't thought about that day in so long. I was only thirteen, and it was the first time I discovered my brothers had developed an addiction to wolfsbane, like so many other great wolves that had fallen before them.

With a sigh, I rolled over, my eyes catching the girl standing just beyond the threshold of the door.

"Zoe?" I asked, blinking through my bleary eyes. *Did she know what happened to her brother? Had she come to confront me about it?*

Suddenly, she was gone, and Frankie had replaced her in the doorway. I closed my eyes once more...

By the time I opened them again, the room was dark. The silhouette remained in the doorway, a black shadow against the light of the hall behind it.

"French," I said, my voice hoarse, "You don't have to stay here. Go home."

"I did go home," she argued. She approached the bed, taking my hand in hers. Even in the dark, I could see she was crying, and I fought the protests in my body to sit up with urgency to fix whatever caused it.

"It's okay," she whispered, laying a hand on my shoulder. She moved to take my hand in hers, placing something small on my palm and closing my fingers around it. I could feel it was a small ring.

My mother's ring.

My ears started ringing as the monitor picked up the increase in my heart rate. *She was rejecting me. Even now? When there was finally hope, and when the truth of our feelings laid bare?*

"I want you to give this back to me," she said quickly, "When I am your mate."

I stilled, my breath faltering.

"And if I am not your mate," she continued, her voice breaking as more tears fell down her cheeks, "Then the ring should never have been mine to begin with."

I felt her lips brush across my forehead, and before I could respond, she was gone.

CHAPTER 21

Connall

A month later, a number of us gathered on the hill, awaiting sunrise. The coven told Noah that with the rising sun, the curse on our bonds would be lifted. I didn't dare breathe as I waited for the first light, unable to offer any words of hope or encouragement.

While others carried on with nervous conversation, creating soft tittering across the hill, Noah and Sophia cuddled together and looked at everyone with blatant hope, filling the air the loudest with their excited banter.

Frankie unconsciously shifted closer to me as she shuffled her weight, her eyes firmly staring at the ground. Her arms were wrapped tightly around her torso as if bracing herself. I wanted to hold her, to tell her it would be okay, but she'd been so distant in the last few weeks since she'd set the firm boundary:

We were either mates or we weren't. If we did not Arrow at sunrise, that would be the final nail in the coffin for us. I didn't bring the ring as Frankie requested, for fear of jinxing it as the gift had the first time.

"It's time," someone amongst the crowd said loudly.

Everyone turned to look at the sunrise, their eyes scanning the skies for something wonderful to occur.

Not me, however. I found myself staring at Frankie, and as if sensing it, her eyes slowly moved from the view to meet mine.

How often had I looked into those rich pools of green and begged the universe to bring us together? After so many moments of longing, I couldn't dare look at anything else.

As the break of orange light reached our eyes, a harsh and cold wisp of air shot through us all.

The moment it hit me, I felt the snap, like a thousand iron ropes springing from my ribs and attaching themselves to Frankie. I almost fell forward from the sudden yank of the bond's pull to her.

She was, and always had been, mine.

"I knew it." I may have said the words aloud as I grabbed her neck and drew her into me. My lips collided with hers, my body bursting into an icy flame from the sensation of kissing *my soulmate, my best friend, Frankie.*

"WAHOO!" I heard the exclamation before an extra pair of arms wrapped themselves around us.

I almost snarled possessively as Frankie broke our kiss, until I heard her jovial laugh at her brother's excitement. Her eyes were wet with relief and pure, unadulterated elation.

I couldn't take my gaze off her, couldn't dare look away in case the bond could break, and I would lose her again. The wave of desire that crashed into me when I saw how openly her gaze proclaimed her love for me was seismic.

Sensing the need simmering within me, the corner of her lips turned upward as she quirked a suggestive eyebrow. "Should we—"

"Yes," I immediately answered before she could even finish the question.

"What?" Benji asked innocently.

We looked at his face, so close between ours, and yet we'd forgotten he was there.

"We'll see you later, Benji," she said with another laugh.

We broke from her brother's embrace and moved quickly from

the crowd, our hands clasping as we ignored the whistles and calls from those we were leaving behind.

But where could we go?

"Why'd we have to hike so far for the damn sunrise?" she lamented as we made our way down the path of the hill, evidently reading my mind.

I pulled on her arm, needing another kiss to assure me this was *real.* She fell back to me with a smile, her arms wrapping around my neck as her soft lips fully pressed against mine again and again. Chaste kisses were not enough, and I slanted my mouth over hers, tilting my head to kiss her at a deeper angle. I was starved for her, desperate to run my hands all over her and never stop feeling her in my embrace.

"We knew all along, didn't we?" Her cheeks were wet with happy tears when we separated. "All those years."

"*Seven years.*" I groaned, gripping her hips tightly as I dragged my mouth down her neck.

"You should've never stopped kissing me on my 18th birthday," she challenged.

"*Me?*" I gaped at her, pulling away slightly, "*You* should've agreed to be with me!"

So much time wasted.

She opened her mouth to argue, and *finally*, I could do what I'd always wanted to in similarly aggravating moments: I silenced her by kissing her with every ember inside of me. She opened her mouth with a soft gasp at my intensity, and my tongue hungrily delved inside.

When my tongue connected with hers, my knees buckled, and I blindly reached out over her shoulder, finding the trunk of the tree beside us to hold us up. We crashed against it and I cupped the back of her thighs, lifting her in the air to wrap her legs around me. With a breathy gasp, her lips fell back onto mine, her fingers raking through my hair as she nipped my bottom lip before licking away the sting.

I pressed my entire body against her, letting her feel all of me and realize that we were not going to lose any more time. The frenzy was overtaking us, and after so many years of desiring her, I would not be able to abstain for much longer.

"Connall," her tone echoed my thoughts, "I *need* you."

"I'll not take you against a tree," I grunted, an assertion we both needed to hear.

"Ugh," she moaned as I worked my lips down her neck, needing to taste more of her skin, "I love it when your accent slips. You only ever lose it with me."

"It's because I can't think straight when I'm around you." I moved to the other side of her throat, continuing my onslaught. "I never have, and I certainly won't ever be able to now."

"Stop talking, Connall, I'm serious. I need you *now.*"

My head was spinning. Frankie deserved as much romance as I could afford her on such short notice... but most of all, she deserved *privacy.*

"My cabin's too far. I might burst into flames before then," I groaned, looking down at her panting chest with a pained expression.

"We can make it if we *run,*" she surmised with a sly grin. She dropped back onto her feet and stepped backward into the shadows of the woods. Before I could ask, she had shifted, leaving her clothes torn and abandoned on the ground.

I shifted and followed her, my heart and head singing at the melding of our minds once we were in wolf form.

We didn't have to hide anything from each other. I didn't need to grit my teeth and control my every thought. Instead, I could sprint freely alongside her, letting my thoughts run wild and twist and tangle with hers like climbing vines on the surrounding trees. I felt her all around me, filling up my senses as I allowed my mind to loudly proclaim my everlasting love for her, divulging just *how much* I'd loved her for years from the very moment I first saw her, riding past the car on her bike.

In turn, she shared all the instances over the last seven years that she desired me, all the fantasies of us that played out in her dreams.

I growled, knowing she was teasing me on purpose.

We made it to the cabin, and thanks to the ranch closing, the area was completely empty.

We were finally alone.

We shifted back, climbing the front steps and laughing under our breaths as I struggled to open the door. The moment she could cross the threshold, she turned around slowly, stepped inside the cabin, and turned on the light, allowing me to take in the full view of her.

As I followed her inside and closed the door behind us, I nearly cried and fell to my knees in worship of her perfect skin and wild hair. Instead, I reached out a hand and embedded my fingers in her curls. I pulled her to me, my arm moving around her waist while my other hand cupped her neck as I kissed her deeply once more. I leaned my forehead against hers and breathed in slowly.

I finally had her. She was mine. I could take my time.

Frankie, apparently, had other ideas. She jumped upon me, her legs wrapping around me with such force that it sent us crashing to the floor.

We didn't make it up from the floor for some time, and it was nearly mid-morning when we finally climbed into the bed. Though we'd stayed up through the dawn and morning, I wasn't sure how much sleep we'd be able to get. It was all true what the bonded had warned us about, the relentlessness of the frenzy that took place after Arrowing. I couldn't tire or get enough of being with her. I could spend years inside this cabin and never need anything else, just *her*.

I was certain the frenzy had to be worse when it was seven years overdue.

Not worse, I mentally corrected as she rolled over me once more, *It was so much better.*

We held each other for a short while after, catching our breaths as she looked around the room.

"Okay," she said finally, looking up at me. "I guess I'll move in, but on two conditions."

"Name them, and it's done," I insisted. The thought of Frankie *in my bed... every night...*

"One, we get some more art put up on these walls. Two, we only live here while we're building the house."

"We're building a house?" I repeated.

"A home," she corrected.

Our eyes connected then, and we moved toward each other once more.

It was much later when I disentangled myself from her long enough to make it to the bathroom. After I dried my freshly washed face, I eyed myself in the mirror, startled to see a reflection I didn't recognize.

There was a light in my eyes I had never seen, a redness across my usually pale cheeks, and I couldn't stop grinning like an *eejit*. *Frankie was my mate, my home.* I had been searching for this much longer than seven years, and I had finally found it.

How often had I convinced myself I didn't Arrow on her because my worthless soul did not deserve her? But she *was* my soulmate, and I *was* her perfect match.

I would spend the rest of my life proving that to her. I opened the bathroom door, taking in the sight of her sitting on the edge of my bed waiting for me, scarcely wrapped in my bedsheet.

"You're a goddess," I said through a thickened throat.

"Shut up, Con." She laughed, but her chest reddened.

I slowly made my way over, kneeling on the floor before her. "I mean it," I vowed as I ran my hand along her leg, lifting her ankle to meet my lips. "Until the day I die, and even after," I whispered, kissing her other foot. I moved between, to the inside of her thigh, giving it the same attention and reverence with my lips. "Frances," I breathed, "I will worship you."

Redness flooded her chest even more as her breaths became panted. "Connall," she said again, her tone a mix of wonder and admonishment.

If I was a heathen for my words, I didn't care. I could not fear Hell when I'd already made it out once and found myself in Heaven.

PART SEVEN

A New Beginning

CHAPTER 22

Frankie

We'd been mated for a month, and I was still getting used to the feeling of waking up in bed with Connall. One of his warm arms supported my head like a pillow. His other arm draped over me like a weighted blanket. His brawny body pressed up against my backside. *His soft lips kissing up my neck.*

"Goddess," he murmured gruffly before he dragged his nose from my nape to my ear with a sigh.

"Hm?" I hummed in reply, making myself sound more sleepy than I truly was.

"Are you awake?" he asked softly, hope edging his tone. I felt his teeth graze over the most sensitive part of my nape, and a wave of goosebumps broke out across my skin.

"Hmm," I hummed again. I kept my eyes closed, but a smile tugged at the corners of my lips, revealing the truth.

He called my bluff and rolled over me, crushing me with his full weight. "How about now?" He smiled down at me, an eyebrow lifted.

Before I could answer, he dove his head downward, conquering my lips in a heated kiss.

I laughed breathlessly when he pulled away to pepper kisses

along my cheek, neck, and shoulders. "You're in a good mood this morning."

"How can I not be... waking up next to you?" he replied smoothly. "Also, I have a good feeling about today."

"Oh yeah?" I moved my hands from where they were trapped to push him off me and get some air in my lungs. "What's so special about today?"

Too swiftly, he moved his knees on either side of me and grabbed onto my wrists, pinning them above my head. "Sorry, French," he said, sounding blissfully unapologetic, "You aren't going anywhere."

"No?"

"Not for a couple of hours, at least." His grin was so cheeky I nearly melted. *Unabashed, seductive, playful Connall. A Connall only I got to see.* "It's all a part of my master plan. What say we clear our schedules for the morning and stay in bed until the afternoon?"

I gasped in mock admonishment. "Con—"

"Do you doubt my endurance? Shall I *prove* to you how insatiable my desire is for you? I think we could beat our record."

A whisper of doubt *did* enter my mind, though it had nothing to do with his seductive promises. It was a nagging concern that had been bothering me for some time:

We were finally soulmates, but we weren't yet engaged. *If he desired me so strongly, why hadn't he proposed yet?* With normal shifter couples, the wedding usually followed mere *days* after the Arrowing. I could accept there was another danger looming over our heads once more, but if we waited for the smoke to clear completely, we might be waiting forever.

And I'd waited long enough.

"You know," he said thoughtfully, leaning back to survey my expression, "I was kidding about doubting me, but the look on your face is damaging my ego."

I laughed again. "Sorry, I was thinking of something else."

"Then I'll have to work harder to keep your focus," he replied, his mouth capturing mine again.

To his credit, it worked. That afternoon, however, my impatience struck me once more. As we strolled down the path from our cabin to the garage, I felt myself becoming increasingly irritated.

"After you do some tinkering, would you want to go for a swim at the lake?" he asked me, his voice full of innocence as he reached his hand behind to lay his palm on my rear.

I swatted his hand away, biting back a scandalized smile. "We are *literally* outside our Alpha's house." Before the Arrowing, I would've never taken him as someone with a penchant for PDA.

"French," he said softly, as if reading my mind, "I was starved of your touch for so long, I don't care if the whole ranch watches me claim what's mine."

Then claim me as your wife, I mentally begged, *Just propose already!*

"Anyway," he pressed, "The lake? Are you up for it?"

"No!" I yelled, reaching my limit.

His spine straightened, the light dimming from his eyes a little. "Oh, that's fine, we don't—"

"I mean, yes!" I corrected, "But also, no!"

"I'm confused," he said softly, blinking a blank stare.

"Where's the ring, Connall?" I crossed my arms to hide the heat flooding my chest.

His neck turned red, matching my blush. "The, ah, the ring?"

"Your *mother's* ring, Connall! The one I gave you in the hospital? Maybe you were still suffering from blood loss and forgot, but when I *gave* you the ring, I *told* you *I wanted it back* if we were soulmates! And we are!"

He rubbed the back of his neck, avoiding my eyes. "I remember."

I felt the air flood out of me, the fight within me dissipating into shame. My voice dropped to an embarrassed murmur. "So then why... why haven't you given it back, then?"

A flash of frustration crossed his expression. "Seriously? There hasn't been a right moment, French."

"Oh, *come on*, Con. I don't need a string quartet—"

"We had to rebuild the ranch after a zombie wolf attack! And now Beau's dark witch is being held captive in our wine cellar! Or have *you* forgotten?"

With a frustrated growl, I turned to stomp away from him. Quickly, his hand was on my arm, pulling me back to him as his lips crashed against mine.

I refused to be mollified, taking out all my frustration into our heated kisses. I raked my nails down his back, gripped his face, and tugged at the length of hair I could grasp between my fingers. I realized he was growing his hair long again, and that discovery sent a shiver down my spine.

"Christ, French, you really didn't think I've been planning it?" he asked, his voice gravelly as he tore himself away, "Asking advice from your dad and brother, wanting the day to be perfect?"

That did give me pause. "Really? What did they say?"

He rolled his eyes in a flash of irritation. "Oh, I don't know: A day off of work so you can enjoy a lazy morning, some time spent in the garage, and after that, a visit to the lake. Or something like that."

I froze as his words settled in, the hope in my eyes slowly rising to meet the amusement in his. *He said he had a good feeling about today.* "You mean..."

"*As ucht Dé,*" he groaned, pinching the bridge of his nose with his fingers. "Yes, French. Milo is setting up a bunch of rose petals and candles at the lake *as I speak*, but have it your way!" He dropped to a knee, and I squealed in delight, clasping my hands together.

"*Really?!*"

"*Yes,* really, you *maddening* woman!" He spoke through his teeth, but there was only love in his gaze. "Now, be quiet for a second so I can do this right."

I mimed zipping my lips, an excited jolt going through me as he reached into his pocket and pulled out his mother's Claddagh ring.

The moment I saw it again, tears flooded my eyes.

"Frankie," he said softly, "From the moment you sped past me on your motorbike, I've felt pulled to follow you. Even when our bond was cursed, I knew to the very depths of my soul that there could be no one else for me. If you will do me the greatest honor of my life and marry me, I promise you that in this lifetime and the next, I will follow you, I will—"

A sudden hollering in the distance tore our attention, and we turned to see Benji running at us.

"*Freeze!*" I yelled, holding up a hand to halt him and Noah, who was following behind him. "He hasn't finished!"

My brother dramatically froze with one leg posed in the air. "Well, get it over with already!" he yelled, stomping his foot to the ground when he could hold his balance no longer.

"This family has a real intolerance to patience," Connall muttered under his breath. He looked up at me with a smile. "I'll say the rest later."

The tears broke free from my eyes. "Then I'll say this now: *Yes.*"

With a beatific smile, Connall rose to his feet, pulled me into his arms, and swung me around. His melodic laughter rang in my ears until Benji tackled us to the ground.

CHAPTER 23

Connall

The violins began to swell as I brought my new bride to the dance floor.

I pulled Frankie up against me, one hand sliding to the small of her back as the other held tightly onto hers. "It's about time you fulfill your promise to me," I murmured into her ear as we began to sway.

She pulled back slightly, a challenging grin across her beautiful face. "I beg your pardon?"

"At the last Summit, I asked if you'd dance with me," I reminded her, "You said *whenever.*"

"Maybe I knew to wait until the *perfect* time."

"That's my wife," I hummed thoughtfully, "A picture of patience."

"Say that again," she swiftly demanded.

"That you're patient? It won't make it any less a lie—"

"Not that." She rolled her eyes with a smile. "The first part."

I rested my forehead against hers, grinning. "My *wife.*"

She shivered with excitement. "Yeah," she affirmed, "I like that. Mrs. O'Faolain."

"Or," I said quietly after a beat, "What if I became a Mactire?"

She pulled back to look at me fully. "You'd change your last name like my dad did?"

"I never much felt like an O'Faolain," I answered honestly, looking around the party where there wasn't another wolf with that name, "But Mactire... now, that's a name that feels right in my soul."

She kissed me, her hand grasping the back of my neck to pull me down to her. I surrendered happily, wrapping my arms around the bodice of her dress to haul her up against me.

Our audience whistled and clinked their glasses, but I could feel no shame at all over such a public display.

"I cannot wait until we are alone," I murmured against her lips, "No offense to our guests."

She pulled back with a soft smile, resting a hand on my cheek. "Agreed. But let's keep that just between us."

My throat thickened with our words as I said them. "Just between us."

⟫⟫——◇——⟪⟪

"Alex, Cody, thank you for coming back to Wolfsblood so soon," I greeted my old friends. I'd gotten separated from Frankie in the chaos of chatting with the crowd, and their friendly faces were a welcome reprieve from stagnant small talk with strangers.

"I'm happy for you, man," Cody insisted. "We wouldn't miss this for the world."

"You know I always *suspected* something was going on between you two," Alex added cheekily.

"What gave it away?" I wondered aloud, "Was it the moment I threw myself off a roof to protect her?"

The boys laughed at the memory.

"Yeah, I'd say right about then," Alex agreed.

"Where's your family, man?" Cody looked around. "There's a

surprising lack of *ginger-vitis* in this crowd. I don't even see Noah's mate and I was hoping to tell her some embarrassing stories about him."

"Sophia's around. My dad and brothers couldn't manage the trip, I'm afraid," I said quickly, skirting the awkward truth. I had finally fulfilled my father's wishes, and evidently, he didn't care. Our wedding invitation went ignored. "We're going to visit them for the honeymoon."

"That'll be nice!" Cody offered, not knowing just how wrong he was.

"Excuse me," Adeline's voice interrupted as she approached. She smiled at me, leaning over to murmur quietly, "At weddings, there is typically a mother-son dance. I know I could never claim a space in that tradition, but I thought perhaps—"

Immediately, I offered her a hand.

As Adeline and I made our way to the dance floor, she smiled with tears brimming in her eyes. "I always hoped this day would come."

"Did you?" I asked lightly. "I recall a time you once offered to *command* my feelings away."

"Oh, Connall." Her hand gently patted where it rested on my arm. "Don't you know? There's no Alpha that can *will* the bond away. It took a very powerful witch like Eden just to suppress it. The bond is the strongest magic there is. Even if you had allowed me to try, it wouldn't have worked."

I was stunned into silence.

"In some ways, I hoped you had agreed to let me try the Alpha order," she continued playfully, "Only so that I might put it to the test and affirm my belief that Frankie has always been meant for you."

"Seriously?" I pressed, "You would *test* it?"

"Perhaps not," she replied immediately with a soft laugh, "Either way, the fact that you *refused* was the only sign I needed to surmise that the bond was truly there."

I found myself speechless. *Perhaps, if we had gone to her before the curse was lifted, she would have given us her blessing—*

"Mind if I cut in, Auntie?" Frankie asked, finally reappearing by my side.

"Not at all," Adeline replied. She pulled me in one last time to kiss my cheek. "I don't need to welcome you to the family because you've always been a part of it," she murmured. "But I will say this: I love you, and I'm so happy for you both."

"Thank you. For *everything*," I replied softly as we separated. "I love you too."

A flash of surprise crossed her face, her tears breaking loose as she turned away, and I realized it was the first time I ever told her that.

"You are such a *sap* today," Frankie joked, slapping the back of her hand on my chest. "I wonder, what's gotten into you?"

"I blame *whom* I've gotten into," I played along just before capturing her lips. What began as a playful brush of my lips quickly turned more heartfelt. My hands cupped the sides of her neck, tilting her head as our kiss deepened.

"That was nice," she sounded dazed when we finally parted, "Shall we go hunt down a werewolf now?"

I looked up at the exit in surprise, seeing Noah slip through the back door with a severe look in his eyes. "Our afterparty guest arrived early?"

Frankie raised a single shoulder with nonchalance. "It appears so."

I couldn't be bothered to act surprised. I learned already when it came to us, be it zombies, witches, or werewolves, something wicked would always come.

The difference was now I had a ferocious bride by my side to face it all.

I took her hand in mine, leading her from the dance floor. "Let's go."

CHAPTER 24

Frankie

We eviscerated a werewolf and shortly thereafter set off to make love across the Irish coastline. *The perfect beginning to marital bliss.*

The honeymoon may have started perfectly, but the closer we got to the east side of Ireland, the more the light in Connall's eyes dimmed. His family had an impressive manor at the top of a hill by Wicklow Forest, a dense wood that their wolves could run around undetected, and down by the coastline, his uncle owned a small pub. When the dreaded time came to present ourselves before his family, his Uncle Tadgh was apparently the lesser of all evils to begin with.

An asshole appetizer before the main buffet of bastards, I joked as we got in our small rental car and started the journey.

Connall's mouth only twitched in reply. He had been so open and full of light at our wedding, I hated to see how coming here was pulling him back to the shadows of his former self, turning him back to stone.

The town his uncle lived in was surprisingly small and quiet. I would have thought it *too* quiet were it not for the din of a busy crowd sounding through the walls of his uncle's establishment.

"Is the *whole town* here?" I asked as Connall opened the door for me.

The moment we stepped inside, we were enveloped in warmth, chatter, and music. Connall took my hand and led me past the live musicians and through the crowd to squeeze our way up to the main bar.

I couldn't stop myself from grinning. I *loved* it when Connall held my hand in public. I looked around at the crowd proudly as if to say, *Do you see this stupidly handsome Viking that's holding my hand and powerfully steering us through the chaos of this crowd? Yeah, that's my mate. My husband. Mine!*

I breathed in the scent of the fireplace and beer, distracted by the peculiar sting that hit my nose, as if someone was wearing an extremely strong and earthy cologne that suffocated the air. I lifted my head and looked for the source, noticing the surrounding mustard-colored walls were full of stained and dusty black-and-white photos of wolves.

"Con," I murmured, "Is the decor just an inside joke, or is this a *shifter pub?*"

"Shh," he hushed me in reply, "The townsfolk don't know who they're drinking with."

"Surely they must *guess* when half the crowd doesn't get drunk," I muttered to myself.

As we approached the bartender at the front, I knew instantly that he must be Connall's uncle. He had the same large build, though his age had tamed the fiery red from his hair, leaving it looking a pale copper.

Connall stepped up to the bar, his hand holding tightly to mine as if it were an anchor holding all his emotions at bay.

"What can I get ye?" Tadgh's eyes briefly flickered up to regard us before returning to the glass he was filling with a dark ale. He lifted his eyes again, his hand frozen on the tap. "Connall?" His voice was airy, as if he were seeing a ghost, "What're you doing here?"

"I'm on my honeymoon," Connall replied thickly, "Uncle Tadgh, I'd like you to meet my soulmate, Frankie Mactire."

His uncle dragged his eyes to me with soft wonder. *"Mactire?"* he repeated, "So, your mate was in America, all along?"

Connall and I both frowned at his surprise. *Did they not receive our wedding invitation?*

"I sent word..." Connall's voice was low.

Tadgh cut the tap, the beer beginning to flow over the edge of the glass. He looked around the room quickly, and gestured for us to follow him with a quick flash of his hand.

I swallowed harshly, my heart rate increasing as we moved with him down a short hallway into a vast but dimly lit stock room, full of machines and kegs.

"We should be okay here," Tadgh answered mysteriously after shutting the door. "We only use this space for brewing."

I sniffed in the scent of the hops, and once more it came with a peculiar sting. It suddenly dawned on me what I was smelling: Wolfsbane.

In the beer? I faced the kegs, peering more closely at the labels.

"Connall," Tadgh spoke again, "You shouldn't have come."

"Are you fucking kidding?!" I blurted, unable to hold the words back as I turned back around.

"It's nothing against you," his uncle promised, turning to me, "I truly wish you both all the happiness in the world. But things here have been... well, they're not good." He turned back to Connall. "You haven't seen your dad yet, have ye?"

"No, we haven't," Connall answered, "What's going on? He hasn't answered any of our messages."

"Colm's not in his right mind," Tadgh answered, "He hasn't been for some time. If I were you, I'd leave as soon as possible. Do *not* try to visit him."

"I wasn't expecting a hug welcoming me home, but I cannot deprive him of the opportunity to say *something* about me Arrowing," Connall argued. "I barely know the man anymore, but I *do* know he'd love to declare he'd been right all along."

Tadgh's eyes dropped to his wringing hands. "I suppose it's time you knew," he said after a short pause, "Sending you to America was *my* idea."

I jolted in shock. *And Tadgh was supposed to be the asshole appetizer!*

Connall merely blinked repeatedly at the news. *"Sorry?"* he asked, his voice dropping low.

Tadgh raised a hand in defense. "Now, before you get the wrong idea, I only did it to protect you, as I promised your mother I would in the moments before she passed. Sending you far away from this darkness was the only way to ensure your safety."

"What darkness?" Connall scoffed, "What was so bad I couldn't stay? What about my *brothers?*"

"*They* are already lost, Connall," Tadgh's voice shook as he took an angry step forward, "As is everyone else under the clutches of the Devil's Helmet. It's an epidemic here, Connall, and it's slowly killing us all."

"Even Ceallach?" Connall sounded doubtful, "He never used wolfsbane before."

"Ceallach," Tadgh spoke the name quietly, as if it were a curse. "He's the devil himself. *He* has me infusing microblends of the herb in our special shifter brew to *expand* the illness."

My nose had been right, after all. *Wolfsbane-laced beer.* "Why?"

"He said it was good for business," Tadgh explained, "A pub that brewed and distributed a special kind of ale that kept shifter customers coming back. I've known all along what was the truth. It's for *power* and *control* that expands beyond just our pack. The gardens of O'Faolain Manor is the only place where wolfsbane can be harvested in this area, and they've taken a monopoly over the entire market. Once the wolves are hooked, they're at his mercy."

"So Connall's brother is some evil mastermind that purpose-fully got a bunch of Irish wolves hooked on wolfsbane?" I reiterated, doubt heavy in my voice, "What's Colm doing about all of this as Alpha?"

Tadgh sighed, lowering his head. "My brother-in-law thinks he's the kingpin running the show, but he's too far gone to even realize his power is slipping. Any day now, Ceallach will convince Colm to transfer the Alpha power to him, surpassing all his deadbeat brothers before him." Tadgh laid his hands on Connall's shoulders. "Leave as soon as you can and protect your bride. Colm's hatred for you has only deepened with his illness, and you're the only threat left to Ceallach's throne. Neither your father nor brother will react kindly to a surprise visit."

Connall pinched the bridge of his nose. "I'm the youngest," he argued, "I've never been a threat to Ceallach, or anyone else for that matter. I was a *sap*, as you always said. "

Tadgh gave him a sad smile. "*I* always said you had your mother's heart. I meant that as a compliment."

Connall's hand around mine clenched tightly as he vibrated with emotion. "You all dismissed me from the moment I was born. You cannot claim now—"

"After what they did to your mother, it was in your best interest that I keep your father apathetic toward you. When his opinion turned to hatred, I knew you would only be safe if we sent you away and severed all ties."

"*What did they do to my mother?!*"

Suddenly, the door opened, and Tadgh quickly moved to the side, allowing the large figure to enter. "C-Ceallach!" he greeted, forcing a congenial tone. "I was just tellin—"

"I think you've done enough talking, Uncle." Ceallach's voice was casual and cold. "I'd get back to the bar if I were you; it looks like you have some thirsty customers waiting."

Tadgh left with a quick nod and a final glance of warning to us over his shoulder.

The moment we were alone with Ceallach, he raised a single eyebrow and smirked. "Well... isn't this a happy reunion?"

CHAPTER 25

Connall

"So sorry I missed the wedding," my brother's tone lacked any real apology, "My sincerest congratulations on finding your mate, at long last. Have you come to gloat?"

"*Gloat?*" Frankie echoed, her voice dripping with hatred.

Ceallach's eyes settled on her with severe curiosity. "Now, wait a minute," he said slowly, "Isn't this that *mouthy she-wolf?* She's *actually* your mate?"

"Aye," I affirmed, pulling her a step behind me. "And you will show her some respect."

"But she wasn't your mate at the Summit," he continued, as if not hearing the threat. He broke into a sarcastic pout. "Aw, Con. Did your little Arrow suffer performance issues?"

I growled. "You might've heard, but our entire pack was *cursed* from forming the bond. We were even attacked by the witch who did it with an army of Ripped. Or did *Athair* not get my Alpha's message asking our *supposed brother clan* for their help?"

"Did Uncle Tadgh's ramblings not paint the picture well enough for you?" Ceallach countered, crossing his arms in boredom. "We're a bit preoccupied with a pack of zombies of our own."

"Your uncle seems to think that's *your doing*," Frankie snarled.

"Do not speak of what you don't understand." He flashed his glare to her only briefly before returning it to me. A smart decision, for if he looked at her threateningly for one second longer, I would have pounced. "You should consider yourself lucky. Tadgh worked very hard to poison everyone against you so you could break away to freedom. The rest of us were not so fortunate."

I snorted in derision. "Not so fortunate? From what I hear, you're about to become *Alpha*. It seems *most* fortunate to be our father's favorite."

Ceallach took a threatening step forward, his voice becoming low. *"Athair's favorites* are rolling around in their filth beside him. *That* is what our father does to those he *loves*. His soul is a black hole that sucks you in if you get too close. *Leave now...* while you still have happiness worth protecting."

"This is our honeymoon, and I'm getting really tired of everyone telling us to fuck off," Frankie muttered through her teeth.

Ceallach did not acknowledge her. His eyes remained on me, and I briefly saw a flash of another, more desperate, emotion in them, before it was buried under his usual snide stare.

"Connall," he said, his tone almost pleading, "*Go.* We don't want you to be here."

"Fine." I took my mate's hand and led her back through the bar, reaching the exit. I did not look over my shoulder once and determined if I never stepped foot in my uncle's pub again, I would be glad for it.

"There's a storm coming for us all at the Summit, Connall." I realized Ceallach had followed us out when called out from the doorway. He crossed his arms and leaned against the doorframe, his smile impassive once again. "Enjoy the honeymoon while it lasts. We'll see you back here with the others soon."

"The next Summit's going to be *here?*" Frankie whispered to me with a gasp.

We made it into our hotel room, and as I moved to light the fire at the hearth, I heard Frankie's stomach growl.

"Christ, we haven't eaten," I realized. We had planned to have our meal at the pub, never guessing our visit would be cut so short. I sighed. *I was failing my duty to provide for my wife.*

"I'm okay," she lied, her voice covering another stomach growl as she moved to sit before the fireplace and remove her boots.

"I'll order room service," I promised, moving to the phone.

"Wait," she said, holding out a hand. She pulled me to sit beside her and curled her legs in, facing me. "That was... a fucking lot to take in at once."

"I already knew of my family's dangerous habit with wolfsbane," I revealed, "I just never thought it could become what my uncle says it is."

"Do you truly believe Ceallach is behind it all?"

"I couldn't say," I answered honestly. "I feel as though they are all strangers to me now. I can't make any assertions about what any of them are or are not capable of."

"I guess we'll see how the Summit goes," she muttered, "I cannot believe things are apparently *so rotten* that *we* have to leave, but in the winter, they'll host almost every goddamn shifter on the planet."

I begged for her forgiveness, "You deserved so much better than—"

"Forget *me!* What about the welcome home that *you* deserved?"

I took a deep breath, looking at the rug's pattern as I processed my thoughts. "I never expected to receive the warmest of welcomes," I said quietly. "As a child, our dynamic was anything but *familial*. Even so, I thought if I Arrowed as my father wished, that might change. I never imagined..."

"That everyone else we've met since we got on this island would be more hospitable than your own family?" Frankie finished for me.

I swallowed harshly, looking down. "French, I could not be more sorry for how they treated you. Your family was so welcoming from the start—"

"Our family," she corrected, taking my hand in hers. "You needn't apologize or feel responsible for the behavior of those monsters. Connall... it's me who could not be more sorry."

I looked up in confusion to find her eyes were welling with tears. It gave me half a mind to drive back to the coast and kick the ever-living shit out of my brother for making my wife so upset on our honeymoon.

"I always suspected there was no love lost in your exile, particularly after meeting Ceallach at the last Summit," she said softly, "but I hate to think of all those years *you and I* were forced apart. So much time passed when I tried to hate you or when you pulled away... how *alone* you must have felt throughout it all."

I shook my head. "French, there was nothing we could have done differently."

"There was!" she insisted, "If I had just believed in what I felt between us, I could have been your home from the beginning! I could have found a way, maybe sought out some witch of my own, or even had just run away with you when you asked—"

"Frankie." I moved her hand to rest over my heart, stroking her cheek with my thumb. "You are a welcomed arrow through the heart. The pain means nothing compared to the overwhelming bliss that came with it. I should never have asked you to run away from our family. I cannot imagine our life without them. Everything happened as it should, where we made no compromises on our capacity for happiness."

She rested her forehead against mine with a wistful sigh, not fully convinced.

"I would go another seven years of solitude if it brought me to a night such as this," I continued, "A night where I can watch how the firelight dances in your hair, where I can hold you in my arms, love you with abandon…" I pulled her in and whispered against her lips. "…and know that you are *mine.*"

I kissed her hungrily, an exhale of immense relief escaping my nostrils the moment our lips connected. Whatever darkness surrounded us, Frankie would always be my light. Our kisses became open-mouthed and more desperate, and I felt her hands move to my sweater.

I allowed her to remove it from me quickly, with my under-shirt following shortly thereafter. Her breath increased with her desire as her eyes raked down my chest, her fingertips following the path of her gaze. I loved when she looked at me possessively, her eyes and hands claiming what was, and always had been, *hers.*

"You will never go another seven years like that again," she promised, tugging on the waist of my pants to bring me up against her, "And we are going to make up for all the lost time at *every opportunity* we get."

"Seems fair to me." I grinned before moving her to lie under-neath me.

>>———♡———≪

I dreamt of dark and cold rooms, and when I awoke with a start and found myself alone in darkness, I sat up with the fear my happy ending had only been a dream. My panic subsided when I found Frankie naked and softly snoring on the floor beside me, her hair a mess on top of her head and her mouth slightly parted in her sleep. My eyes adjusted to the darkness and I saw what remained of our quickly-devoured meal was still on a tray beside us, Frankie's outstretched hand just inches from the final slice of toast.

Had she fallen asleep reaching for it?

I smiled to myself, uncertain as to when we had worn ourselves out into sleep entirely but knowing for certain it would not be long before we incensed each other again.

As quietly as I could, I moved to step out onto the balcony and admire the hotel's vast gardens below. The sky was a brilliant cerulean, a color promising a new day dawning.

I breathed in the chill of the coastal air, bewildered we would be returning to these lands so soon. After this visit, I thought I would feel ready to let go of Ireland once and for all... but perhaps it was not quite done with *me* quite yet.

I would be returning to my homeland in a few short months with my new clan by my side, ready to defend ourselves against whatever threat came for us.

Mactire was my last name now, and I would fiercely protect it.

Coming soon...

※———♡———※

Released
The Fifth and Final Book Of
The Arrowed Series

※———♡———※

Acknowledgments

Picture this: you are in a sandwich shop, eating your new favorite sandwich that's become your current obsession, and the person you're with (who you imagined you'd dedicate many years of your life to) dumps you without any prior warning there had been anything wrong in the relationship. As you chew your sandwich and choke back tears, you find yourself feeling completely distraught and blindsighted.

Imagine how that sandwich might taste the next time you try it.

Now, imagine that you are actually *me*, that sandwich is actually this novella, and the person who dumped me is actually the company I worked for at the time I was just beginning to explore Connall and Frankie's story.

Convoluted metaphor to say... I may have never returned to this work were it not for the readers and fans of the Arrowed Series who supported me through one of the scariest times of my life, spread the word about this series, and emphatically encouraged me to publish the next one.

This "sandwich" is for you.